So We Can Glow

So We Can Glow

STORIES

Leesa Cross-Smith

THORNDIKE PRESS
A part of Gale, a Cengage Company

LIBRARY OF CONGRESS CIP DATA ON FILE.
CATALOGUING IN PUBLICATION FOR THIS BOOK
IS AVAILABLE FROM THE LIBRARY OF CONGRESS.

ISBN-13: 978-1-4328-8448-2 (hardcover alk. paper)

Published in 2020 by arrangement with Grand Central Publishing, a division of Hachette Book Group, Inc.

Printed in Mexico
Print Number: 01   Print Year: 2020

For your (girl) eyes only,
from Eve until the end

CONTENTS

WE, MOONS

We're not depressed all the time, some of
us aren't even depressed sometimes. We're
okay, our hearts, dusted with pink. When
we cry in bathrooms together it's about men
or our mothers or our fathers or our bodies.
We are resilient, none of us have attempted
suicide, although we do at times imagine
what it would be like to have never been
born. Is that sadness? Is that regret? We love
men. We are ashamed of this attraction. We,
the ones who aren't lesbians or asexual,
wish we were; we fantasize about lesbian
communes or asexual communes. We take
the curse of Genesis 3:16 to heart. Isn't it a
curse to want a man? Didn't God intend
that after the fall? We *feel* cursed. We are
Eve. We develop crushes on men we'll never
meet, men in magazines. We prefer our men
to remain onscreen where they cannot hurt
us. We, protected by those alien-beams of
light, that space glass. We envision those

men down on their knees before us, looking up at us, smiling. We pat their heads and call them good boys. We use them. We crave and *desire* them. We leave them whether they want us to or not. We wear their clothes because they smell like them and we let the sleeves hang long past our wrists. We swear to one another we won't call or text them during our Girls' Weekend. We try to keep our word. We try really hard. They call us, they text us, they send us pictures of the flowers they'd have delivered to us if only they knew where we were. We are in the mountains or on the beach or at a grandmother's home; the grandmother has passed and left it to us, left us her journals and her cake recipes, left us the blankets and sweaters she knit, the quilts and tea-stained books she read when she was young like us. We are not *young,* but we are younger than our grandmothers. We are young enough to still have our periods. We bleed together when the moons are death-darked and new, ovulate under the full ones. Their fierce, primal, ancient names connect us to the women who came before and all those who will come after: wolf, snow, worm, pink, flower, strawberry, buck, sturgeon, harvest, hunter's, beaver, cold. If we had been in charge of naming the moons, we wouldn't have changed a thing. Some of us are mothers, some of us have miscarried, some of us have no desire to bear children in our dark and starry wombs. Where do we go for emotional rescue? Where do we go to feel safe? Where do we go to escape the men who would rape and murder us, the men who would kidnap us, the men who would torture us, the men who would, the men who, the men. We are complete without them but we want them anyway. We love them but we want to hide from them. We drink champagne and wine and whiskies and stay up too late smoking. We eat dark chocolate brownies and coconut cakes and wake up and fry eggs with butter and chilies. We lock our doors at night and keep our secrets. We howl at the moon and paint our toenails with glitter and make promises, free before we leave. We return to our homes and our children and our jobs. We return to those men, the ones who keep us, the ones we are afraid of, the ones who would never harm us, the ones who protect us. We know they desire us, they are cursed with wanting to be inside of us. We are wild and cannot be tamed. They are cursed with wanting to tame us. They want us to be witches so they can burn us. They burn with lust for us. We use our own lust-flames to fuel us and keep us warm. We are better at this than they are. We read and write our books, sing our songs, scream our screams, and fall easily into the arms of a God who loves us. We fight a God who loves us. We beg for forgiveness for we know not what we do. We know what we are doing. We run away and want to be found. We want to disappear. We want to be seen. We search our breasts for lumps so our breasts won't kill us, our cervices for tumors. We scan our bodies for poison, never knowing. We feed our babies with these bodies and offer our bodies to the men we desire and the men take and take and take and we give and give and give. We are handmaidens and helpmeets and neither of those things. We are created in the image of a God who can be both man or woman or neither. No empty vessels; we are achingly full, spilling over. And when we die, our souls pour out like water.

THE GREAT BARRIER REEF IS DYING BUT SO ARE WE

Minnie and her husband Adam were unusually quiet on their way home from the theatre. Adam was the actor, the star. Adam *had* to kiss his costar Caitriona during the play because it was in the script.

"Did you want something to eat?" Adam finally asked.

"I don't care," Minnie said, staring out the window.

"Chinese? Greek? Maybe a burger?" Adam asked, pointing to the restaurants as they passed them.

"Well, too late now. There they go," Minnie said, fussily flicking her hand and waving to the restaurants, their signs. Shadows of people. Lurking. Waiting. Too hungry or too full.

"I can go back," he said, tapping the brake gently. Slowing.

"Nope. I'll eat something at home."

"Are you angry with me?" he asked as he

let off the brake, gunned the car forward.

It was late. A Thursday night hinting at a stormy early morning. As they'd walked out of the theatre, the sky had been a black-violet dream. The diamond stars, out just long enough to evoke wonder, were now hidden with the moon.

Minnie went into her purse, felt for the cool chunk of rose quartz in the little zippered pouch. Right there next to the earrings she had taken out after they got too heavy. Right there next to her three favorite lipglosses. The colors made her hungrier. Grape. Tomato. Peach.

"I'm going to practice downstairs when we get home. I mean, sorry if you need to sleep, but I need to learn this piece," she said. Minnie played cello in a string quartet. She was playing a wedding tomorrow night. Her best friend, Stella, one of the violinists, had composed a new arrangement of a Nat King Cole song for them to add to their repertoire. It was the summer wedding season and the next four weekends were booked.

"That's fine. I understand," he said.

She wrapped her fingers around the crystal, loving the weight of it. The flats, the points.

"I know you get upset sometimes when I

16

have to kiss Caitriona —"

"It's your job, right?" Minnie snapped.

"Yes. It is my job, but I don't want you to be upset —"

Adam spoke softly, came to a full stop at the sign before turning right. They were ten minutes from home.

"What does her mouth taste like?" Minnie asked, looking over at him.

Adam made a noise. Not a sigh. Something wearier.

"Minnie, I don't *taste* her mouth. It's a stage kiss. It's a totally different thing," he said.

"I know what a stage kiss is," she said.

"Okay, then you know it's not like a *sexual* thing. We are *pretending* to be lovers. Caitriona plays my wife. That's all."

Minnie's stomach growled so loudly it hurt.

"But the two of you dated before, so it's not all pretend," Minnie said, using air quotes around *pretend.* She was effectively annoying herself and could only imagine how Adam felt about her at that moment. He probably wanted the car ride to be over like she did. Adam ran a yellow light, which endeared him to her. She could never be attracted to a man who would stop as soon as a light turned yellow.

"Twenty years ago, Minnie. Cat and I dated *twenty* years ago and we didn't even sleep together. You know this. We've been over this. It's exhausting," Adam said.

You're exhausting is what he meant. And she'd never believed they hadn't slept together anyway.

Adam and Caitriona had dated in the nineties and that was what made Minnie the most jealous. Caitriona had known him then, when Minnie hadn't. There was a picture of them Minnie had pinned to the walls of her brain, couldn't untack it even when she tried. Adam, with a red-plaid flannel tied around his waist, his black-framed glasses not unlike the pair he wore now. Caitriona, next to him in her flowered Doc Martens and ripped jeans. They were at a Pearl Jam concert and Adam was smoking because he smoked back then. Caitriona was wide-mouthed, surely laughing at something Adam had said. Adam was funny in the nineties and Adam was still funny now. But now Adam was forty-five, not twenty-five. Now, Adam was a father and an AP History teacher. He and Minnie had a twelve-year-old daughter, a thirteen-year-old marriage, a thirty-year mortgage. He and Minnie had met right as the nineties

18

were dipping out and Y2K fears were slipping in and every time she thought about that picture, she felt like she'd missed out on something in his life before her. Caitriona had known Adam when he was a smoker, when he had beery breath, when he tied flannel shirts around his waist and listened to music, not just NPR. Caitriona had known Adam when they were both learning the lyrics to *RENT,* when Adam had played Roger in the local production. Caitriona had played Mimi. While Adam was living his superstar-laidback-local-theatre life, Minnie had been in school, getting her music degree with a cello emphasis.

Cat. Minnie hated when Adam called Caitriona *Cat.*

Minnie was cultured too. One of her cello teachers had called her a rare talent once and Minnie had almost wanted to get it printed on a sticker and slap it across her orange hard case.

Minnie felt mousey in the passenger seat. She glanced at Adam. He looked tired. They'd go home, pay the babysitter. Adam would have a small glass of whiskey and ice before taking off his glasses and rubbing his eyes, falling asleep on the couch watching one of the West Coast baseball games while

Minnie played her cello downstairs. She was angry with him and knew how ridiculous that was. She still wanted to have sex with him. Minnie's stomach growled again.

"So, you're on hunger strike because I get paid to kiss Cat every night? You think I don't ever get jealous of you and Connor going all over the countryside together, playing at these romantic events like some kind of . . . sexual troubadours?" Adam asked, pushed his glasses up.

"Sexual troubadours? Really? Wow," Minnie managed to say before laughing loudly.

"Absolutely, sexual troubadours. You and Connor drinking wine and rambling through the forest!"

Adam stopped at a red light and looked at her.

"*Rambling* through the forest? With a cello? Adam, for the love, give it a rest. Oh and don't forget there are two other women with us . . . it's a quartet!"

"More like a duet," he said.

"Really? You think we, what, use a time machine and go back to the High Middle Ages every weekend?"

"Caitriona and I have been working together for years. You know her. I barely know anything about Connor."

"You know plenty about him!"

"I know the guy plays the viola, that's all."

"He's been to our house, you've met his wife."

"I don't taste Cat's mouth when I kiss her," he said as the light turned green.

"*You're* exhausting," Minnie said to him, before he could say it to her.

Adam paid the babysitter and did everything Minnie knew he would do. She went upstairs, changed into her pajamas, came down and sat on the other side of the couch, put her arm around Ivy who was nursing a small mug of chamomile like an old woman. Adam had the ballgame turned down low and sipped at his whiskey. Minnie had reheated last night's ziti and cheese and finished it, standing in the kitchen. Adam had made himself a roast beef and cheddar cheese sandwich, the crusts bordering the small plate he'd balanced on the arm of the couch. Minnie looked at her phone, saw a text from Connor. A question about the new music. She put it down without responding.

"Daddy, who are you for?" Ivy asked. Her voice was sleepy. She sat on Minnie, snuggled up to her even tighter. They'd been attachment parents, Minnie slinging Ivy wherever they would go when she was a baby, breastfeeding her until she was two

21

years old. Ivy had slept on Minnie exclusively until she was five months old. Because of that, Ivy tended to sit on Minnie or Adam, like she was hatching them. Minnie felt a bit guilty being overstimulated by it and made sure she set aside some time at night to let Ivy sit on her, knowing it wasn't Ivy's fault they'd raised her that way. Ivy especially loved perching on Minnie when she was sleepy.

"Tonight? Let's go with the Rangers," Adam said. He was a Cubs fan but they weren't playing.

"I'm for the Angels," Ivy said.

"Me too," Minnie tacked on.

Adam looked at them, drank his whiskey.

"You should never root against *angels,* Daddy," Ivy warned.

"Of course not," Adam said, giving up too easily.

"Ivy, scoot off to bed. I have to practice downstairs," Minnie said.

"But I want Daddy to tell me about the play."

Ivy got up and plopped into Adam's lap. It was his turn to be hatched.

"Ten minutes," Minnie said to both of them before getting up and going downstairs.

Minnie closed the basement door, got out her cello. She ran through the pieces they always played at the weddings, the pieces she could play in her sleep, to warm up her fingers. Tchaikovsky, Bach. In between, she heard Adam's deep voice murmuring upstairs, followed by Ivy's giggles and conversation. Minnie pulled out the new sheet music, stared at it until her eyes went out of focus, until the black notes slipped down the white page and blurred away. Ivy tapped gently on the basement door and Minnie told her to come down.

"Night, Mommy," Ivy said, hugging her neck.

"Goodnight, pigeon." Minnie put her arms around her daughter, kissed the top of her head.

Ivy went up, closed the door again.

Minnie had taken her phone downstairs in the pocket of her pajama pants. She pulled it out and texted Connor.

Wanna FaceTime this new piece?

She imagined Connor in bed already, his wife sleeping next to him. Minnie pictured his face, lit up with the phone light, reading her text. She rosined her bow, tuned. Waited for Connor to text her. If Adam had ever come right out and asked Minnie if she had a crush on Connor, Minnie would have told Adam yes. But Adam hadn't asked. Adam wasn't even particularly jealous. Everything he did was a reaction to Minnie, her jealousy. And Minnie liked to lean into the lion's mouth of her jealousy, let it snap shut.

She was in the lion's mouth when she got a response from Connor.

Fuck yeah!

She smiled, looking at his *fuck yeah.* Exclamation point. She thought of his mouth shaping the words and her thighs warmed.

She considered Adam dozing off on the couch upstairs, his glasses on the small table next to him. She could hear the low mutter of the TV, the baseball commentary, the rhythmic clapping. Something important must've been happening. Minnie pulled her hair up, a sloppy bun at the crown, smoothed the strays behind her ears. She was wearing an old T-shirt she'd gotten on their honeymoon, now ratty and worn, with a big faded pineapple on the front of it. It was her favorite, the softest. She answered when she saw her phone screen light up.

"Heyyy there, Minnie Mouse," Connor said.

"Hey," she said, wondering if Adam could hear her or if he really was sleeping. She thought about going upstairs to check but decided not to.

She could see that Connor was wearing a ratty T-shirt too and a pair of sweatshorts. Minnie's desire flickered at the intimacy of it. Connor usually practiced in his basement too. His was finished like theirs, with cushy carpet and a row of paperbacks and college textbooks behind him.

"You want to play it together to see what we've got?" he asked.

"Okay," she said, suddenly feeling quiet. She'd wanted to see his face on her phone, she wanted to play, but now she was tired. Tired of everything.

"I was drinking a vodka tonic. A vodka tonic with lime," Connor said.

"Are you drunk?" she asked.

"Off *one* vodka tonic? I'm offended."

"Well, I don't know how many you've had!"

"Oh, Minnie Mouse, are you in a fussy mood? Have you eaten?"

"Yes, I've eaten! Stop that! I'm fine," she said, laughing lightly.

"You're the WORST when you're hangry," he said, readjusting his camera so he could sit in his chair properly. He put his viola

25

underneath his chin. He looked buzzed, his hair bed-headish. She'd seen him buzzy and drunk before and easily recognized the familiar wide, sheepish grin.

"Are we going to play this or are you going to bug me instead?"

"I may be a *little* drunk," Connor admitted. He let his viola rest on his knee, looked right into his phone camera. He made a tiny space between his thumb and forefinger.

"Asshole," Minnie said.

Connor lifted his viola, put it under his chin again and played the beginning of the new piece perfectly. Minnie watched, listened. Then he played Beyoncé's "Halo" for her too. They played it together at weddings sometimes. It was one of Minnie's favorites. Afterward, Connor put his viola on the floor next to him, picked up his phone, looked into the camera.

Minnie covered her face, turned the phone away.

"Hey, are you okay? What's going on?" Connor's voice said out at her.

"Nothing. I'm fine," she said. She was crying. She sniffed.

"Well, turn the damn phone around so I can see you please. You don't sound fine. Wilhelmina!"

She wiped her eyes, turned the phone around.

"Wilhelmina, why are you sad?" Connor asked. He relaxed his body, leaning back and balancing his left ankle on his right knee.

"I'm not. It's the song."

"Where's Adam?"

"Upstairs." Minnie used the collar of her shirt to wipe her eyes some more.

"What else are you thinking about?" Connor asked.

"Nothing."

Minnie sniffed again and with her tender, wavy, cry-voice, told Connor she wanted to run through the piece a couple times. So they did and they sounded lovely together. It would sound even better tomorrow with both violins. Minnie and Connor sat there looking at one another for a little too long.

"All right, little Minnie Mouse . . . I guess I'm going to hit the hay," Connor said as he put his viola in the case. Minnie caught a glimpse of the plush, gold lining. He lay down on the floor, his head leaning against his hand.

"Connor, do you think Adam is having an affair with Caitriona?" Minnie asked, lowering her voice and leaning closer to her screen. She blew her nose and left the tissue in a small, tight ball next to her foot. She turned, double-checking the basement door, knowing full-well Adam slept like the dead. Connor didn't know-know Caitriona but he'd seen her around enough at the theatre, the art center, the city.

"What?" He shook his head.

"You heard me."

"No, I do not think Adam is having an affair with Caitriona."

"Do *you* want to sleep with her?"

"Do *I* want to sleep with Caitriona?"

Minnie tilted her head to make sure she couldn't hear Adam upstairs. No. But she lowered her voice even more.

"You know what I mean . . . is Caitriona the kind of woman a man would have an affair with?" Minnie asked, knowing it was a ridiculous question. Anyone could obviously have an affair with anyone.

"Are you wondering if I find her attractive?" Connor asked.

"I guess . . . yeah."

"Are you wondering if I find her more attractive than you?" Connor asked.

"What? No!"

"Sure you are. You're asking me whether or not . . . as a man . . . I'd want to trade *you* in for a woman like Caitriona and the answer is no," he said.

Minnie stared at the screen and watched Connor blink at her. He smiled, blinked. They were quiet together, connected by the electric-blued light.

"You're only saying that to make me feel better."

"I'm not," Connor said, folding his arm behind his head, adjusting his phone.

"I thought you were going to bed."

"I was! But then you started flirting with me so I got a second wind," he said, laughing.

"Connor! I was not! Go to bed," she said.

"No. You go to bed."

"Where's Samantha?" Minnie asked after his wife.

"Asleep."

"Where are the boys?" Minnie asked after his sons.

"Asleep."

"Tonight Adam called us sexual troubadours."

"Wait, what? Called *who* sexual troubadours? You and me?" Connor sat up, laughed again. Connor was always laughing. It made Minnie laugh. She put her hand over her mouth before shushing him and turning her phone volume down.

"He said we were more like a *duet*. He only said it because I was jealous of him

29

kissing Caitriona . . . in the play."

"Aaand because they used to date."

"But never slept together," Minnie mumbled.

"But you never told him *we* slept together," Connor said.

Minnie's toes twinkled.

"That was a long time ago," she said softly.

"Right," he said.

It happened one night after a wedding, traveling. The quartet was three hundred and fifty miles away. The women got one hotel room, Connor got another. The other two women had gotten drunk and fallen asleep. Minnie was sober, awake, went across the hall to Connor's room.

It was one of those nights Minnie was feeling lonely although she hadn't been alone much in days. Ivy was always either sitting on her or underneath her or Minnie had been giving cello lessons to the middle schoolers she always gave them to, or she and Adam were either next to one another in bed or next to one another on the couch or next to one another in the kitchen. But Adam also had rehearsals, work, more rehearsals. He and Caitriona had just begun rehearsals for the play they were in now.

The play that had a total of two cast members.

1. Adam.
2. Caitriona.

Minnie truly believed Adam was in love with Caitriona even though he denied it and even though he was always good to Minnie. She couldn't shake it, like she had an allergy to *not* believing it. And she didn't want to talk to Connor about that, but she wanted to be close to someone. Adam was three hundred and fifty miles away at home with Ivy. Sometimes when Minnie played weddings they got a babysitter and Adam came with her, the two of them driving home together in the dark, her heels slipped off and cornered on the floor of the car next to her black, slick-footed stockings.

She tapped on Connor's door and he opened without asking who it was — the luxury and privilege of being a man.

"Minnie Mouse! Fancy meeting you here. What's up?" he said, his voice bright with alcohol.

"I can't sleep," she said.

"My room is your room," he said, ushering her in. He closed the door behind them.

Connor was handsome in a sneaky way.

31

His teeth were a bit big and his mouth had to do some extra work to cover them. His eyes were unremarkable, the color of chili. He looked like a computer-generated version of a man. Something aliens would create to explain humans to one another. Something plain enough to get the point across, but nothing too special. That was the sneaky part. The more Minnie looked at him, the more time she spent with him, the more handsome he became. Like one of those magic pictures that revealed something even deeper, even more important, if you looked at it long enough and let your eyes go out of focus.

"You're a night owl too," she said to him and meant for it to be a question, but it didn't come out like one. It made her more insecure, the fact that she couldn't even ask a proper question.

"Sometimes. Samantha is the early bird," he said. There was one bed in the room. Connor sat against the headboard, crossed his feet at the ankles. He was wearing his glasses and usually wore contacts. He was wearing a blue Cubs T-shirt, which made her think of Adam, except she was already thinking of Adam, so it felt like wearing a wet bathing suit in the rain.

Minnie didn't know where to sit. They

were friends, had been friends for years. Close friends, even. But it wasn't like she was used to being alone in hotel rooms with him. There was a chair and a desk. She pulled out the chair and sat there.

"Is it creepy if I say you can sit on the bed?" Connor asked.

"No. You're not a creep. It would be creepy if you were a creep. Besides, I came over here. It's not like you showed up at" — she looked at the clock, read the time aloud — "twelve forty-five in the morning at *my* hotel door claiming you couldn't sleep. I'm the aggressor here."

"What are you aggressing, Wilhelmina?" Connor asked. He smiled. Connor smiled a lot.

"You're the only person in the whole world who calls me Wilhelmina. Not even my parents call me that."

"It's a pretty great name."

Minnie shrugged, got on the bed beside him. He looked at her.

Minnie was shocked at how easy it was to kiss Connor. One moment they were making jokes about some random commercial and the next, Minnie had her head on Connor's shoulder. So when Connor turned his head to look at her and leaned forward, they were kissing. Almost like an accident.

Once Connor was on top of her, there was a moment when he stopped kissing her, pulled away, took his glasses off and extended his arms so he was hovering over her.

"Are you sure this is okay?" he asked. Her mouth tasted like his — the pepper-metal of vodka, the bright, starry bite of lime.

"Are *you* sure this is okay?" she asked him.

"Samantha and I have kind of an open relationship thing. She has a guy . . . a man . . . she sees him sometimes. I don't ask too many questions," he said.

"Adam and I —" Minnie started, then stopped.

"Yeah?"

"This is okay," she finished, nodding.

Connor and Samantha's open relationship thing meant Connor had condoms. Minnie tried not to think about the other women he did this with. How often? How many? One? Five? One hundred? He was a pharmacist and Minnie thought about that when he was inside of her. She pictured him in his white coat, the name tag. She'd seen him in it a couple times when she went to the drugstore where he worked.

She opened her eyes and saw the pinched vertical line between his. *I am having sex with Connor. I am having sex with the viola*

34

player. I am having sex with a pharmacist. I am having sex with a man who is not my husband. I am having sex with not-Adam. She wondered if Connor saw the periodic table when he came, if he thought about metals and gasses, if he anxiously double-checked his brain to make sure he hadn't screwed up someone's prescription. He made a dove-like sound when he finished — a quiet, gray coo. Minnie laughed after she came. Maniacally in a burst. Connor shook his head and laughed with her, gently pulling the hem of her shirt down for her as she put it back on. Connor went barefoot to the vending area and brought back one of every candy bar — sugary-chocolate sticks of peanuts and nougat and almond and coconut and milk chocolate, dark chocolate — and they ate them in bed together, watching a documentary about the Great Barrier Reef.

"Everything is dying," Minnie said as they watched the neon-green fingers of a sea anemone wiggle in the water. Glowing hot-purple, blue, and pink corals, crookedly stacked like dirty plates in a kitchen sink. She licked chocolate from her fingers and began to cry as the smack of a shock-yellow fish moved through the ocean. Connor pulled her close, touched the back of her neck and let his hand stay there.

"You're okay," he said. He said it again, softer.

Minnie snuck back into her room in the early morning hotel hallway light. No one knew what had happened but the two of them, not even Stella. And at breakfast, the only things Connor did to acknowledge it:

1. maintain eye contact while he took his shoe and purposely tapped the top of hers as she sat across from him putting jalapeño cream cheese on her toasted bagel

and

2. put his hand on the small of her back as they left the hotel. A light touch, like a feather blowing by. The wind?

Yes, it happened once. And sleeping with Connor was the worst thing she'd ever done. Couldn't everyone see it? Didn't the green-haze fug of it pulse from her skin?

Back in her basement, with Connor's face on her phone screen, Minnie considered these things and simply said again, "That was a long time ago."

"Well, about six weeks ago," he corrected her. Frowned.

"Let's talk about something else. Like, how I wish I had a cup of tea."

"What kind?"

"Rooibos and honeybush with a wedge of lemon and a smidge of sweetness."

"If you were here with me, I'd make you that cup of tea."

"Would you?" she asked.

"You know I would," Connor said.

Minnie took a deep breath in, tried to keep herself from crying and said, "Okay, I'm going to bed."

"So am I," he said.

Neither of them budged.

Neither of them looked away from their screens until Adam opened the basement door and Minnie jumped and ended the call.

"Sorry I startled you," Adam said, yawning.

"I'm done down here," she said.

"Good. I fell asleep. I couldn't even hear you."

"Go to bed. I'm coming up in a sec."

"Love you."

"Love you, too."

When Adam was gone, Minnie texted

Connor.

Sorry! It's fine! I was just jumpy. Adam came down here. Thanks for practicing with me tonight. See you tmrw. X

He responded quickly.

No worries. Until tmrw. Goodnight, Minnie Mouse.

Minnie went upstairs, scrolled through Adam's phone. There were no texts from Caitriona. Minnie was disappointed and felt foolish for that disappointment, which made her feel even worse. She was a black cloud, a sunken ship. She washed her hands at the kitchen sink, stood there drying them, staring off at nothing.

She got Caitriona's number from Adam's phone, beeped the digits into her own, and typed:

I know you're in love with Adam. I know it. And trust me, I get it.

Minnie stared at those words, those letters, those symbols representing whatever they represented, in the language they both knew. She sent the text, then deleted it from her phone. She went to the bathroom, washed her face, flossed, brushed her teeth. She went into her purse and put that rose quartz on her nightstand. She didn't *believe* in crystals, but she liked knowing it was there. She took off her clothes and got into bed with Adam. She'd tell him about Connor soon. And maybe he'd tell her the truth about Caitriona too. Soon enough. Maybe Adam knew about Connor already, the same way she already knew about Caitriona. Minnie fell asleep quickly, only to gasp awake with anxiety fifteen minutes later. Her heart, tap dancing. She arched her back and cooed like a dove, relieved when her husband reached over and moved her hair — his fingers, her nape, the lown dark.

UNKNOWN LEGEND

She wanted to work in a diner because Neil Young sang about it in "Unknown Legend." That romance. That wistful, dusty harmonica. Her hair wasn't blond, it was black. She changed the words whenever she sang the song. Turned *blond* to *black* with her voice, like a witch casting a spell. But no, she wouldn't like to ride a Harley-Davidson because motorcycles scared her. Her ex had a motorcycle and she used to ride on the back of his, but that was different because he made her feel safe. He'd turn around a lot at stop signs and red lights and say, you're okay. And she liked how he said it without the question mark. He *told* her she was okay and she believed him. She believed him as much as she believed in the very air she breathed.

She'd moved to the desert towns seeking magic — Joshua Tree, the Mojave, Taos. She loved all of them. Deserts sparked her heart.

She didn't like to stay in one place *too* long. How could she be an *unknown* legend if she were *known*? She got a tiny cactus tattoo on the inside of her wrist, a small crescent moon above it. She'd told the tattoo artist it was her fortieth birthday and that she had promised herself she'd get a tattoo on her fortieth birthday. She never broke her own promises. When she walked out of the tattoo parlor — her smarting, tender wrist in the sun — she went to the drugstore to buy an expensive matte nude lipstick, a cheap glossy one too, so she could compare. She also bought two bottles of white wine. She was forty and it felt like a very *forty* thing to do. So did going back to her apartment with her new tattoo and putting on her pajamas and watching *Law & Order: SVU* with Thai take-out and her wine.

The diner wasn't far from her apartment. She could walk there in the morning, but she didn't like walking home alone at night. She drove herself to the night shifts, drove herself back home with the tall yellow-white lamps strobe-lighting up the inside of her truck. Flashing, flashing. Sometimes she'd think of her motorcycle ex and wonder if he was still married. Where did they go wrong? How could love silently fall away like a petal, without them noticing?

There was one new cook at the diner she liked enough. He was quiet and gentle, so unlike the other men she'd known and been with. She didn't want a boyfriend for the same reasons she didn't want a pet, but the *idea* of a husband was nice. Someone who smelled good, someone who would cut their grass once she saved up enough to move out of the apartment, once she decided to stay put for long enough to buy a house. She would be a *known* legend then. *Known* by her husband, a man. A man who would lie underneath her truck with only his legs sticking out and push himself up with black grease-dirty hands and wink when he told her he'd taken care of things. He'd fixed it. Whatever it was. Fixed. A man with a spirit as kind and calm as Neil Young's ghostly, barely-there voice. A man whose spirit made her feel the same way Neil Young's songs made her feel. *Autumnal. Dreamy.*

There were two diner customers she liked well enough. One was a trucker, always passing through. And he'd say it as she put his coffee on the counter, his eggs and toast. *Passing through.* He'd told her he liked to sit at the counter for company. He'd told her the road was lonesome. He was divorced and bearded. His kids were in college. One morning after her shift, they'd gotten a booth and had some coffee together, but she didn't tell him anything deep about herself. *Unknown.* She remained a mystery. She promised herself if he came back three more times that month, she'd tell him something that third time. So far it'd been only two.

The other diner customer was the man who owned the hardware store across the street. A cozy little spot that smelled so good, sometimes she'd go over there on her breaks and wander around. He was definitely married and deliciously off-limits, but he was so nice and tender-hearted, she couldn't help but be drawn to him. When he came in the diner, he didn't sit at the counter. He sat at a booth by the window. He wasn't lonely. He didn't need the company.

One day, she saw him crying in the booth. Not sobbing, but wiping his eyes, looking at his phone. And when it was time for his refill, she approached him carefully. Poured. Asked if he was okay. And he told her he was fine. He'd be fine. It was just that he and his wife had thought their young son was sick, really sick, and his wife had texted him from the hospital and told him the tests finally came back clear. He was crying from relief. He'd been at the hospital with them early that morning and only left to open the hardware store, to keep it open. And he'd given himself ten minutes to take a break, to come over and have a cup of coffee. He hadn't had a day off in months, he said. He said his wife couldn't call him yet, but she would soon. He said his wife and son would be going home. He couldn't stop talking to her in that booth and she loved it. She sat across from him for a little bit, took her break right there with him and listened to him talk about his son, show her pictures. She'd miss him most of all when she left. She had to leave. It was how she'd stay *unknown*.

But she told herself she wouldn't leave until the trucker stopped back in for the third time that month. And when he stopped back in for the third time, she'd tell him something she hadn't ever told anyone else and then she'd leave. On the last day of the month with the clock almost running out, he stopped in. *Passing through.* She asked if he would mind if she took her break with him. Asked him if he'd like to get a booth with her. He said yes.

He was surprised she knew how to drive a stick shift. He liked that she was from Kentucky. He asked if she'd grown up riding horses. They talked about Neil Young

44

and how she always listened to *Harvest Moon* when the harvest moon was full. A superstition. He said he'd start doing it too and think of her. For good luck. She asked him to show her his truck and when they went outside to stand next to it, she put her hand on his stomach. Touched him, gently. Told him she loved the desert towns, that she was still waiting for that magic kiss. And she cupped her hand around his ear and like she promised herself, she told him a secret. Something she'd never told anyone else. His beard was brushing against her face — soft soft soft — when he was squeezing and hugging her, so sweet and tight.

LOW, SMALL

We were a dying wasp. The only thing I still liked about him was the shape of his nose when he was looking down. *Not enough.* He would get his words twisted around when he was upset. He'd say gold bright instead of bright gold. Light the turn on instead of turn the light on. Tiny things, which kept his anger small. *Small.* In bed I curled into a catlike C, tightened myself to the edge. I was on a boat lost at sea — there was fog, there was rain. I made a C, I was lost at sea, I couldn't see. He was careful not to touch me, afraid I would scream. There were nights when I would've screamed and other nights when I would've let out an ocean-water sigh, a beckon, a beacon of sound. *Low, small.* When he came inside from cutting the grass, my husband wove a thick ribbon of good-stinky animal musk from the back door to the bedroom, from the bedroom to the shower. It was leathery, whiskey and wood. Beard and muscle, it was breath and sweat; it was a swallowing shadow of man and men. A darkening cloud, a cup emptying and filling up. His hulking enormity, made slight. It brought me back to him — a smoky, creepy, long, sharp-nailed cartoon finger. I met him in the hallway and told him our love was decoration. We wore it like jewelry, slipped the thin posts into the holes in our ears, slid slim goldbright bands over our wrinkly knuckles. We were deep-green parsley on a runny-yellow dinner plate. Garnish. I took his rough hand. Led him to the teeming backyard gardens where the bees hung and swung. Hovered low, small. "Our love is sad. We need to *grow* it," I said, stretching my arms wide, wider. Widest. Titchy fireflies winked neon light around us, the grass was summer-soft beneath our bare feet. I approached the blinding goldbright throne of a God I'd made low, small; I prayed for efflorescence.

A TENNIS COURT

Down there, they always peed outside. Hush-slipped their dress hems from their knees to their waists and squatted. Alabama girls. Alabama roses. *What a pretty name: Alabama Rose,* Leigh thought. The words swung down behind her eyes as she pulled her underwear back up where it belonged. *Georgia Rose.* That name was in the song they were just dancing to. The song playing in the reception tent. It was a song by one of those foreign boy bands, their mouths and faces lemony and light. One of the boys had hair the color of the inside of an apple, all lit up and glowy. She liked the curly-haired one best because he looked like a little prince.

Michael looked like a little prince too. The girls walked back to the tent and saw him. The groom. He had his wedding suit coat hooked on one finger over his shoulder. He was dancing to another song now, something she'd never heard. The girls resembled an outrageous, drooping hydrangea bush standing there bunched up together, smelling like sweet cocktails and fruit; they'd had peach cranberry lime strawberry cherry pineapple with vodka gin bourbon ice and sticky lipglosses to match. Michael had a brother named Wolfgang and their parents had a tennis court because anytime you named your kid Wolfgang, the baby came with a tennis court. Wolfgang looked more like a Daniel or a John. Michael looked like the Wolfgang and because of it, the entire family was upside down. None of them made sense. The mother wore too much yellow, the father talked way too loud, the brothers didn't look enough alike and they also had a sister who was far too young, like she'd taken a crooked turn, wandered into the wrong family. But she was decent enough so they kept her, not knowing what else to do. They had so much money, nothing mattered anyway.

Michael and Jill were the newlyweds. Leigh and Jill worked together at the court-house. Of course Jill had invited the court-house girls and there they were, standing and sitting and drinking and eating and dancing when they weren't peeing. Alabama girls. Alabama Roses.

Wolfgang's brown-sugar eyes stuck to Leigh's and he asked her to dance. She said okay and he said not here . . . on the tennis court. She said okay again and finished her champagne, motioned to the courthouse girls. They were supposed to keep an eye on one another. Fine. Done. Okay. She was keeping an eye on herself.

She followed Wolfgang's stalwart body. He'd been a college quarterback. Or maybe it was baseball. Leigh couldn't remember, didn't care. They were kissing on the dark tennis court, the smooth pleasant warmth of it heating up the backs of her thighs, her calves. She slipped off her shoes, little honey-colored heels covered in flowers. Everything was flowers. Midsummer in the South was an explosion of flowers. *Bonanza!*

"You didn't come with anyone?" he asked.

"I came with my girlfriends," she said.

"I meant, a *man,*" he said, moderately annoyed. It made her like him more. It was a treat to annoy a man so easily.

He kissed her earlobe, the milky pearl stuck in it.

"Do you play tennis?" she asked.

"Sometimes."

"You played in college?"

He nodded against her neck. It wasn't football. It wasn't baseball. It was tennis.

50

She thought of her old crush on Pete Sampras, her current crush on Roger Federer — his wristbands, his responsible eyebrows, his celebratory hands in the air. She'd always had an affinity for tennis players. Notoriously and gorgeously tall, preppy and competitive.

"What's that bush called?" she asked him, pointing.

"Are you serious?"

She pushed him away, gently. Like peeling off a sticker.

"That one. It's so pretty," she said.

"Crape myrtle," he said easily, turning.

"I know those are gardenias," she said, pointing to the other side where the creamy blooms spread lustily, almost inappropriately wide. Insolent. Forget Alabama Roses. Alabama Gardenias were her new heroes.

"Wow. You're something else," Wolfgang said.

"Your name is Wolfgang," Leigh said. The bubbly champagne laugh had snuck up on her. A bright poppy hiccup leapt from her mouth.

"You're drunk," he said, rolling off her. He sat with his hands clasped, his knees resting against the inside of his elbows. She liked it when a boy sat like that. A man, a boy, a dude, a guy.

"You look more like a John. Or a Michael. You should be Michael, Michael should be Wolfgang. Your family is kind of fucked up," she said, smoothing her hair. Her breath: his hoppy beer and Italian cream cake.

"That one is called abelia. The hummingbirds and butterflies like it a lot," he said, pointing at a bush of white star-shaped flowers. "And bottlebrush buckeye," he said, nodding to the bushes beyond the fence. It was too dark to see but Leigh could feel the rough shrubby beasts slouch in the gloaming.

Leigh closed her eyes and pictured every flower every bush every vine every tree every root every green or brown or white or yellow or red or pink or purple or orange thing snapping and whipping loose and wrapping itself around her, around both of them, suffocating them as they gave their ghosts to the petal-scents and thorns. It's not that she wanted to die but sometimes she would think, *Can't we just get it over with?* It, meaning everything. Everything happening all of the time. She could invent a new cocktail and call it This Exhausting Life.

Two vodka cranberries
Two glasses of champagne
Incalculable humidity

52

The moon — full, new,
or waxing crescent
Wolfgang, cake kisses
The same flippy melon-colored dress,
three different summer weddings
ATTN: HEART
Don't shake
Don't stir
Just, stop

The wedding DJ was repeating songs now. Back to Van Morrison. She could hear the bass, the occasional birdlike drunken whoop. She didn't miss the courthouse girls. She and Jill weren't that close. She hated weddings. Ceremonies, in general. And don't get her started on funerals.

"I think I saw winged sumac back there where I went to pee," Leigh said.

"Yep, there's a bunch back there," he said, nodding.

Nope. No, she didn't come with a man. She wondered if he came with someone. She remembered seeing him with a woman, but maybe she was making that up. Everything *before* was on the other side of the champagne curtain. She brazenly lifted one of her arms to smell underneath. It still smelled like her flowery deodorant. Calendulas. Even in this humidity, even in this heat. Wolfgang was on this side of the curtain and he was looking at her, smiling. Surprisingly agog. He was delightfully half-annoying, half-cute. Thorny enough.

Outstanding — a boy called Wolfgang, a boy on a tennis court.

Irresistible — a boy smart enough to surprise her, a boy who knew the names of the bushes.

If we were snowed in at an antlers-on-the-wall bar somewhere. If the colored lights were low, dancing and swooping at our feet. And something like "Mammas Don't Let Your Babies Grow Up to Be Cowboys" was playing, the sound swimming around us like swirly cartoon smoke, would you stand up and sway with me? Tell me I'm the prettiest girl you've ever seen? Hold my hand real close, tucked in between us like a little animal we wanted to keep warm? I can get real quiet and hardly say anything, but when I got a little buzzed I'd talk to you about my shows. About my crush on Raylan Givens in that cowboy hat. And about how Tim Riggins would've smoked, damn straight. No way would he not smoke. He'd put that unlit cigarette between his teeth, his hair hanging down in his face; his plaid-flanneled arm would reach out for his brown bottle of Texas-brewed beer and he'd talk about touching God. He'd light the cigarette, fire-orange-sparkle-crackle and hush. You know what I'm talking about. How I can't stand lies. How if something is even the tiniest bit wrong, I feel like it's my job to do all I can to fix it. Make it right.

Your mama let you grow up to be a cowboy, I'd tell you, keeping true.

If the rest of the world disappeared in some melty, apocalyptic flash. If we had to live in that bar with those taxidermic timber wolves and red foxes watching us drink and move through candlelight. And after making hot ham and cheese sandwiches over fire in the kitchen and me, standing on the table singing Patsy Cline, would you call me *woman* and promise not to leave? Tell me you're not like other men? Hold my chin, kiss my honey mouth, lay me down on the pool table? I can get chatty and anxious after cold coffee, and I'd ask you where you thought everyone else went. Heaven? Hell? No way would they all make it into heaven. No way would they all burn in hell.

What a relief to not be scared to death of you, here alone, I'd tell you. *That's why the only men I give my heart to live in my TV.*

Woman, I'd never hurt you. I'd die first, you'd say.

And if we were the last two people on

Earth, I'd go cold knowing you were a liar, but I would have to love you anyway. Like all the women who came before me — back to Eve caught in the cool copse. It's sick, I promise.

SURREPTITIOUS, CANARY, CHAMOMILE

We'd moved to Arizona because of my allergies. It wasn't working so far, but I lied to Luke when he asked. And I lied to myself when I turned the air filter knob from three to one.

Luke's morning breath smelled like rust. I didn't mind it in my face.

"You should start to feel better. It's drier here," he said from his side of the bed, as if he were discovering gold — holding out a crinkled, thin pan of nubby nuggets. "It's the desert air."

I didn't have any friends yet. I got so bored while he was at work painting houses, while the twins were at school — before the three of them came home in the afternoons smelling like their days.

Luke: coffee, paint, and sage.

The girls: fruit-scented erasers, crayons, and hand sanitizer.

Sometimes I'd stand at the kitchen window, take forever to do the dishes, watch the homeschooled brown boys swimming next door. They were halfway through high school, as slim-jim and long-legged as colts. Sometimes I'd take forever to water the Kool-Aid-colored geraniums and lantana. Watch the woman across the street come out at the same time every morning in her visor and flowery garden gloves, her collared shirt and pale candy-heart-pink pleated shorts.

I wandered in the dry heat, went shopping. Bought a hat.

"It's good for the sun," the man at the store told me. I had lived long enough and been married long enough to know men were always telling women what they already knew. I nodded kindly and wouldn't let him give me a bag. I put the hat on before I left — the brim so wide it made me feel like a mushroom.

I stopped for allergy medicine. Beer and a pair of new sunglasses too. I tore the tag off and put them on, pointed to the blackheart lenses.

"They're good for the sun," I said to the cashier without smiling. That's what I always did when I was annoyed, passed it off to someone else. Like, *tag you're it.* Gave it away like it was the Cheese Touch.

I chased the antihistamine down my throat with a smooth river of so-light-it-was-basically-nonalcoholic beer I'd poured into an empty coffee cup. I sat in carpool and waited for my babies to come out of the school gym, to fill the back of the car with their secret language and giggle-bubbles.

Over oatmeal dinner, I told Luke I wanted to have another baby.

"If it's a boy let's name him Gunnar. Or Shotgun. Make this whole desert cowgirl thing a reality." I blew off my finger guns and laughed, looked across the table at our twin second-graders named after twinkling jewels.

"I'm already jealous of the new baby," one of them said.

"I'll hate him," the other one said.

"Don't say that," Luke and I said at the same time.

"Jinx!" the girls squealed.

We drove out in sunset-glory, got Jinx Coke Slushies for dessert.

I sat on the edge of our bed wearing nothing but a pair of lust-red suede wedges and my new hat. The air filter, a peaceful plastic monster in the corner, humming and humming. I was reading one of Luke's nature books, underlining the words I liked with a hideous yellow pen. *Surreptitious. Canary. Chamomile.* I meant it as an act of aggression. Rebellion. Claiming my territory, pissing on a bush. Luke never wrote in his books. I whispered the words to myself. *Surreptitious. Canary. Chamomile.* I loved how they made me feel . . . my tongue and lips and teeth, quietly tip-tapping.

"Hey, Brooke," he said. He rarely said my name. Hearing it bloomed my heart, creeped fresh yellow-green ivy up and around the bone cage protecting it.

"Hey, Luke," I said as he closed the door. I'd already checked on our sleeping girls to make sure they were still breathing.

"Do you want to stay out here or go back home?" he said. Was he sad? I didn't want him to be. Selfishly, I wanted to see him smile. Wanted to light the firecracker-swish of his happy face. The sex was always better when we were both in a good mood. I wanted to do this right. I wanted my Arizona Baby — to have him cowboy-swagger right out of me with a tiny gun on his hip. I was ovulating. Maybe that was why I was feeling so dizzy and lonesome.

"I'm naked and you're asking questions." I pouted.

"I'm sorry. I'm worried about you," he said. Cloying. I told him to stop. Told him

61

he was giving me a headache. I shut him up by writing *surreptitious, canary, chamomile* in his mouth with my tongue. He pushed me back and I spread across the bed slowly. Like a flag unfurling on the Fourth of July. Like every damned army in the world was watching, standing to salute.

WINONA FOREVER

Limerence. As if someone had smeared my life lens with dewy Vaseline, I got this dreamy, floating feeling around Crystal. I loved that her name was Crystal. Like, her mom thought the word *crystal* was pretty so she named her that. Crystal's sister was Amber. Of course her sister was Amber. *Was.* Because Amber's boyfriend got drunk one night two years ago and drove his car into the river with Amber in it. No one knew exactly what happened, but everyone knew two eighteen-year-olds shouldn't die. That kind of thing never made sense anywhere, to anyone. Crystal wore a necklace with Amber's picture in it and sometimes when it was late and we were in bed together talking and making lists with the TV on, I would touch Crystal's neck and open the locket and look at Amber staring back at me with glossy lips and those same Winona Ryder–brown deer eyes Crystal had. And we'd cry

63

and cut ourselves together sometimes. Go to her bathroom window and open it, hang our heads out far enough so we could share a cigarette.

I was obsessed with Winona Ryder and got my hair cut the way she had it in *Reality Bites*. It'd come out the year before and Crystal and I had been to see it three times already at the cheap theatre. My mom had taken us to see *Mermaids* in the theatre when it first came out. Amber went with us too and when we were walking out, my mom had told the three of us we reminded her of Winona and we told her she reminded us of Cher, because she did. I didn't have any siblings and Crystal and Amber were the closest things I had to sisters. When Crystal and her family lost Amber, I didn't feel *outside* of them like it was something I couldn't understand because I wasn't blood-related to them. Crystal and I had been friends since kindergarten, I'd known them both almost my entire life. It was like I lost *my* sister too. Crystal and I both got obsessed with Winona Ryder because seeing her onscreen made us feel like we'd been hanging out with Amber again.

Lucas, Beetlejuice, Heathers, Welcome Home, Roxy Carmichael, Edward Scissorhands, Little Women. I especially loved

64

Heathers because my name was Heather. And sometimes when I was in front of the mirror, Crystal would point to me and my reflection and go, *look, Heathers!* It was a dumb joke we loved. Sometimes everything about my life felt like a dumb joke to love. Amber's death drew us closer to one another, and we were already close. But now, we never even spent a weekend apart. We watched the Winona movies in Crystal's room with the door closed because it bothered Crystal's mom the way we watched them over and over again. Crystal's mom thought Winona looked like Amber too, but it wasn't comforting for her like it was for us. Crystal had a big bedroom with her own bathroom and a TV and a VCR and a stereo. We could do whatever we wanted in there, like it was our own apartment. At my place, we could watch the Winona movies in the living room because my parents didn't mind. And my dad's best friend worked at the video store, so he would hook us up and give my dad sweet deals when we bought the VHS tapes. I had them on a shelf in my bedroom because they were as precious to me as my books. Crystal and I shared the collection, but the movies stayed at my house. We had a pact that we'd never watch the Winona movies alone, only together.

And even if one of her movies happened to be playing on TV, if Crystal wasn't with me, I'd close my eyes and change the channel or leave the room completely.

Crystal and I would write WINONA FOREVER on our arms sometimes. Sometimes on our feet if it was warm enough to wear sandals. The boys we liked asked us what it meant, but we wouldn't tell them. WINONA FOREVER was ours and ours only. We liked boys and we liked each other too. Crystal and I kissed when we slept in the same bed. We kissed until we couldn't kiss anymore, but that was all we did. Kissed. We kissed and kissed until our sticky-lipgloss mouths tasted exactly the same. Like cherries or strawberries or pink or grape or blueberry or lemon or Dr Pepper and then we rolled over on fire. Burning and burning before we fell asleep. We didn't tell the boys about this either. Not even when they were being pervs and wanted to get off on asking us if we ever made out. We were coy when we said no, stop it, no.

We started kissing after Amber died. It was summer and Amber and her boyfriend had been out celebrating her boyfriend's birthday. It was summer when Amber and her boyfriend went missing for two whole days until the cops found the car in the river. It was summer when Crystal's family had to bury Amber. It was summer when Crystal and I went and bought all the yellow roses we could find at the grocery store and put them on Amber's grave because yellow roses were Amber's favorite. And we each kept a yellow rose for ourselves and came back to Crystal's room and watched *Mermaids* because Crystal said she wanted to watch something cozy so I went home and got my tape and brought it back. A lot of Crystal's family was still over at her house, in the kitchen, eating and cooking. Her dad was out on the front porch, drunk with his brothers. Her mom was in the kitchen smoking and crying with Crystal's grandmother. Crystal and I went to her room and closed the door and turned the movie on. I put my head on her shoulder and I'd already cried so much I didn't think I could cry anymore, but I sobbed. Again. And Crystal was playing with my hair. I got up and went to the bathroom, blew my nose, washed my face. My eyes were all black and streaked from my makeup afterward. Crystal had taken off her black velvet dress and I took mine off too. We were in tank tops and panties and when the movie was over we got in bed. We could hear her family in the rest of the house, on the front porch, in the backyard. Everyone was being quiet, but the house was somehow loud because it was full and alive, something Amber wasn't anymore.

Crystal looked at me and put her hand on the side of my face and it was both of us. Both of us leaned forward and kissed and kept kissing. My stomach, our tongues — pink cotton candy, swirling. We touched feet in her cool sheets and I don't know how long we kissed with the windows open. When we were finished, we cried some more before Crystal got out of bed and went into the kitchen to steal a cigarette from her mom's pack. Her mom had drank a lot and took some pills and passed out on the couch in her black dress; her dad was out there staring at the TV. Crystal's uncle was at the sink, sniffing and quietly doing dishes with the wet spoons clinking and catching the zappy kitchen light.

I had a headache from everything, but I smoked with Crystal anyway. She peed in front of me, put the seat down and sat there with her knees under her chin. I let my cigarette hand hang out the window whenever I was holding it. Crystal pulled a half-empty bottle of peach schnapps from underneath the sink. We'd absconded with it that morning from Crystal's parents' liquor cabinet. We'd learned the word *absconded* in English class. It was extra credit on the vocab quiz. Cherry schnapps was my favorite, but I liked the peach too. Crystal's favorite was peach. I thought it was important for her to have her favorite that sad night. And I wanted to be there for her, for whatever she needed or wanted. After we finished our cigarette, we went to Amber's abandoned bedroom, touched her stuff, hugged her stuffed animals and cried some more. We didn't sleep much that night and when we ended up in Crystal's room again she and I kissed some more, and I was genuinely surprised when the sun rose, like the night should've been extra-long since everyone was so devastated. The gravity of Amber's death was weighing us down, so why not the sun too? Crystal and I cut ourselves together in the morning. Same spot on our upper thighs, stinging and bleeding; we put on fresh *Little Mermaid* Band-Aids and watched *Mermaids,* finishing off the bottle of schnapps in her room and getting drunk pretty fast because we hadn't eaten. And when we puked, we barely had anything to puke up. We both took showers, washing our hair with the same Herbal Essences shampoo every girl at our school used that fluff up against the boy-smells of gym, weed, and matte Drakkar Noir.

"My breath smells like a funeral," Crystal said. "Winona Ryder looks *so* much like Amber," she said again before she fell asleep in full afternoon sun. I brushed my teeth twice before I went home.

I was jealous of the boy Crystal liked, but that wasn't fair because I liked a boy too. Crystal liked Jamie and I liked Tristan. Jamie and Tristan were best friends. They lived in the same neighborhood, so we'd drive past their houses sometimes to see if they were home, to see what they were doing. Crystal's mom hadn't let Crystal get her license even though it'd been two years since Amber died. She didn't like her riding in the car with me that much either, so we didn't let her know how much we drove around. My parents had gotten me a little white hatchback I loved and Crystal and I called it the white rabbit after one of our favorite songs. I kept our flower crowns hanging around the rearview mirror and we'd put them on whenever we drove past Jamie and Tristan's houses. We thought it was good luck, that it would help us be able to see them, that they'd be out in their yards. Sometimes it worked. We went to school with Jamie and Tristan, but we got a special thrill when we saw them *outside* school. Once, we had our flower crowns on and Jamie and Tristan were out in Tristan's driveway skateboarding and listening to Nirvana. The whole thing was so nineties, so grunge. Jamie even had a flannel shirt tied around his waist.

"Hey," Jamie said, walking over to the white rabbit. He stuck his head in a little and was so close to Crystal I thought she was going to die. Her shorts were really short and we weren't cutting ourselves anymore, so there were no Band-Aids, just a couple pale, smooth scars. I looked down at her pretty legs, her purple-glittery toenails and flip-flop feet on the floor of my car.

"What are y'all doing tonight?" I leaned over and asked.

Tristan came over to my side so I turned to him. My car was sitting right behind the driveway, out of the road. I turned the engine off.

"Skateboarding," Tristan said.

"What are *y'all* doing?" I heard Jamie ask Crystal, but I didn't turn around. I was looking at Tristan and his big brown eyes and my sadness flipped on because I thought about Winona's Bambi eyes and Amber's Bambi eyes. Tristan asked me if I wanted to smoke with him, so I got out and leaned on the hood of my car while he lit my cigarette.

"My parents are in Florida," Tristan told me. "And I like this," he said, touching my flower crown. Would the good luck be doubled or go away completely now that Tristan had touched it? Only time would tell.

"Thank you," I said.

Crystal and Jamie were talking to one another quietly, almost like they were already dating. I could tell Jamie liked her by how he looked at her. I saw him reach out to touch her necklace and Crystal let him. She didn't even flinch and my jealousy ratcheted up, but dropped down low after I pulled my car up Tristan's driveway and we went inside and Tristan kissed me for the first time up against the wall in his kitchen with Crystal and Jamie sitting right there in the living room.

"You're cool with this? Because I like you. I like you a lot," Tristan said with his hand pressed on the wall next to me. The ice-maker in his humming refrigerator rattled. I would've had sex with Tristan. I wanted to. But I hadn't had sex with anyone and I was waiting. For something. But I decided in the kitchen that I would lose it to Tristan whenever I was tired of waiting.

"I like you a lot, too," I said to him before he kissed me again. Was Crystal jealous of Tristan kissing me? When we went back to the living room, Crystal and Jamie were making out on the couch and neither of them even noticed us, so we went to Tristan's room and closed the door.

That quick, I decided I was tired of waiting and I wanted to lose my virginity with Crystal in the same house, so we could talk about it later. I hoped maybe she was in the living room losing hers to Jamie. In *Mermaids,* Christina Ricci almost drowns while Winona Ryder is losing her virginity up in the bell tower, so before Tristan and I did it, I went to the door and opened it and peeked out at Crystal and Jamie. They were under a blanket and I could see Jamie's ass moving up and down. Underneath him, Crystal had her head thrown back, her hair hanging down the side of the couch like a waterfall, her eyes closed. Jamie looked right at me and the look on his face was *placid.* Another extra credit word from our vocab quiz. Jamie looked at me and looked at me, then closed his eyes tight, let his head hang down, and kept moving under the blanket.

Tristan and I moved under his blanket too. Watching Crystal and Jamie made me

73

so horny I felt like I'd pass out. Tristan had been looking for condoms in his dresser while I was watching them, so I didn't even know if he knew what I'd been doing. I liked Jamie looking at me when he was with Crystal like that, because it made me feel close to Crystal. And even when Tristan was inside me with the condom on I was thinking about how later Crystal and I would go back to her house or my house and watch a Winona movie and kiss when we got in bed. I loved being with Tristan. He was sweet and gentle and kept asking me if I was okay and I was. I was more than okay. The night was perfect and the cigarette I'd share with Crystal later would be perfect and seeing Winona's brown eyes on the TV would be so comforting to both of us. We'd talk about the boys, cry about Amber, watch Winona and write WINONA FOREVER on our arms and kiss some more. We'd be cranky with lust and twinkle like sometimes-sad, crooked little lights.

GIRLHEART CAKE WITH GLITTER FROSTING

POSSIBLE INGREDIENTS: Too much black eyeliner. Roses. Champagne from a can, champagne in a bottle. "Music to Watch Boys To" by Lana Del Rey. Pink, lavender cigarettes. Flower water, flower crowns. "Formation" by Beyoncé. Glossy lips, glossy eyelids. "Fetish (feat. Gucci Mane)" by Selena Gomez. Red lipstick. Lipgloss in your pocket, lipgloss in your purse, old lipgloss lost and found under the couch. Lipgloss that smells like birthday cake, lipgloss that smells like blueberry, lipgloss that smells like mango. Your natural hair. Lorde humming at the beginning of "Yellow Flicker Beat." Fairs and beers. Los Angeles, Nashville, Kentucky. Malibu! Miranda Lambert and a lighter. "Milk" by Kings of Leon. Expensive skincare routines. *The Virgin Suicides.* "Don't Dream It's Over" by Crowded House. Green-green summer grass and ice-blue pool water. Lindsay Weir dancing in her bedroom to "Box of Rain." Sunflower sunshine, golden. "Thirteen" by Big Star. Rihanna as fairy godmother. Zazie Beetz. Harry Styles in a wallpapery, wildly patterned suit. Chipped polish and a mood ring. Beach breath, sunscreen. Taking your bra off, finally. And bleeding and bleeding and bleeding. Dresses and leggings and cowboy boots. "Damn I Wish I Was Your Lover" by Sophie B. Hawkins. Vanilla. Cherry. Every Fiona Apple. Lens flares. Kissing your black- (or brown- or red- or blond- or no-) haired husband or boyfriend while he's sleeping, kissing your black- (or brown- or red- or blond- or no-) haired husband or boyfriend when he's awake. Pink quartz, amethyst, carnelian, aquamarine, red jasper, plum jasper, citrine, amber, padparadscha sapphire, etc. "The Summer I Was Sixteen" by Geraldine Connolly. "Dancing Queen" by ABBA. "Killer Queen" by Queen. Feather earrings and hoop earrings and groupies. And Taylor Swift. Father John Misty and Father John Misty's hands in the smoke and lights. Jeff Buckley. Clementine and honey. Patsy Cline. Cool, green iridescent lake water, beer can bonfires. "Spice Night" by Catherine Bowman. Sparklers, twinkle lights, pale sugar. Glitter, glitter. Jefferson Airplane. Ring Pops and Blow

Pops and eyeshadow names. Looping cursive, folded paper. En Vogue and Tori Amos. Heart. Baseball, *A League of Their Own*. Denise Huxtable. Angela Chase. *Felicity.* Keri Russell. Dorothy Dandridge, Eartha Kitt, Barbra Streisand, Audrey Hepburn. Cher. Marilyn Monroe movies. Swish-swishy prom dresses, heels in hand. Lemonade. *Lemonade.* Buzzing neon. Confused hearts, blooming hearts, broken hearts, full hearts. Ale-8-One and church camp, crosses. Peach pop, root beer floats, Popsicles. Jane Austen and Emily Dickinson. Mary Shelley. Judy Blume. "Work It" by Missy Elliott. "Bossy" by Kelis. Shaving legs in kitchen sinks. Secrets, spilled like wine. *Pretty in Pink.* Accidental girlfriends. *Stealing Beauty* and *A Bigger Splash* and *Call Me by Your Name* — every summer obsession movie — panting, drinking, licking, blazing. Oprah Winfrey. Hayley Williams + Paramore. Serena Williams. Roxane Gay. Sylvia Plath. Jenny Lewis. "Does He Love You?" by Rilo Kiley. The Supremes, The Ronettes. "Then He Kissed Me" by The Crystals. Bubbly pineapple water, tank tops, Juicy Fruit. Tegan and Sara. Amy Winehouse and Janis Joplin. Ella Fitzgerald dancing in a black dress next to Frank Sinatra. Judy Garland singing "a big fat rose" to Gene Kelly. Etta James singing "It's a Man's Man's Man's World"; Etta James singing anything. *The Thomas Crown Affair*'s chess scene kisses, Steve McQueen spanking Ann-Margret in *The Cincinnati Kid*. Phoebe Waller-Bridge. Villanelle's pink Molly Goddard dress in *Killing Eve*. Sandra Oh. Natalie Wood. Elizabeth Taylor, Maggie the Cat. Joshua Tree. Antonia Thomas. Sissy Spacek. Sissy Spacek's wardrobe in *Badlands*. *Rookie* magazine. Zendaya. Bonnie Raitt. Stevie Nicks. Indigo Girls. Linda Ronstadt singing "You're No Good." Aretha Franklin singing "Respect." Carly Simon singing "You're So Vain." Tammy Wynette singing "Stand by Your Man." Loretta Lynn singing "Fist City." Margo Price. Princess Diana and Jackie O. Meghan, Duchess of Sussex. Catherine, Duchess of Cambridge. Eve and a pomegranate. Mary, mother of Jesus. Mary Magdalene. Bathsheba. Deborah. Esther. Queen Vashti. *Dirty Dancing*. "Love Is Strange" by Mickey & Sylvia. Sylvia Robinson. Chaka Khan. "This Tornado Loves You" by Neko Case. Coconuts, strawberry shampoo. Alanis Morissette's *Jagged Little Pill*. Lace. Velvet. Mesh. Tulle. Your bedroom — a candy-colored, starry-ceiling sanctuary. "Free Fallin' " by Tom Petty and "American Girl" by Tom Petty and The Heartbreakers. "American Girls" by Counting Crows. "Around the Way Girl" by LL Cool J. Your natural blush, Lolita. Orange Crush. "Cherry Bomb" by The Runaways. Flirting and bar lights. And everysingle heart-dark or heart-light muddy tomboy and frilly girly-girl and bad girl and good girl (and walking the edges, nowhere and everywhere in between), living or can-never-*really*-die dead.

DIRECTIONS: Warm. Or chill. Icy, even.

Fast as You

I was getting paid to watch Tucker's two-year-old daughter Emmylou while he was on stage singing and some other times too. He and his band were on tour. But no, I wasn't getting paid to get in my bunk on the tour bus after I put Emmylou down in her daddy's bed and pull the curtain closed and put my hand between my legs and think about Emmylou's daddy touching me. Slipping between me the same way he slipped his cigarette between those strings of his guitar and let the smoke go and go while he was tuning and getting it right.

Tucker was one of those guys who smoked even though he worked out every day too and kept an eye on what he was eating. It didn't make no sense and that's kind of how he was. He didn't make no sense and I didn't want him to. He wasn't my man, he was Shay's. Shay was a big country music star too and had legs like Jesus had sculpted them with His bare hands, said they were good. Shay wasn't Emmylou's mama. Emmylou's mama was a mystery. She didn't much want to be a mama, Tucker had told me about her. I gave Emmylou extra love because of it and Tuck loved her plenty enough for two. I'd put her hair up in two little pigtails to make her look like a ladybug and wonder how her no-good mama could leave her behind.

Sometimes Shay would be up there singing with Tucker and I'd be standing off the side of the stage holding little Emmylou on my hip with her big, pink, plastic earmuff on to block out the loud sounds. Tucker and Shay had a duet burning up the radio stations and on the nights I was strong and not too jealous to listen, I'd stand there and watch them. On my weak nights, it would hurt my feelings and I'd turn me and Emmylou around right before Shay walked out. Emmylou and I would take the long way back to the bus — catch the sky right as it was changing from late-ombré evening to full-on night black. Every single star shining bright as God.

Tucker wasn't an easy flirt. I had to earn it. Like the time I put on a turquoise feather skirt and went next door to his hotel room to pick up Emmylou before the show. He opened up the door and I sang the chorus of "Amarillo by Morning" to him and wasn't the tiniest bit shy about it because I'd been practicing in the shower. That part was easy to sing once you listened to the song all the way through just once. I'd listened to it about five hundred times. That was where we were headed after the show in Oklahoma City. Amarillo. Tucker looked me up and down and did a cartoony wolf whistle and he never did stuff like that, so you got to hear me out when I tell you it was really *something.* Emmylou was toddling around in her overalls, babbling behind him. Tucker was saying look at you. To me.

"Damn right about Amarillo by morning. I'm ready to get back to Texas," he said.

I wanted him to say more about my skirt, but didn't want to make it too obvious or desperate. I bent over and got on my knees, opened my arms for Emmylou to run into them. I got Emmylou's bag and Tuck closed the door behind us. Emmylou and I were going down the hallway, walking hand in hand in front of him and I had a feeling that little skirt looked best from behind. I thought about him thinking about me, thinking about me differently than just Emmylou's nanny. Thinking about me the same way he thought about Shay. Thinking about my body and my legs and what was under my little skirt. And I was thinking about his arms in his shirt, how I cut off the sleeves for him those nights he was on stage sweating and singing. His perfect, cute-fat ass. And those nights when I'd put Emmylou to sleep at his place and he'd be downstairs writing music and wearing those gray sweatpants that made me want to fall out and die. Those nights, this life when I'd give any damn thing for him to take me to his bed. For him to take hold of my hips and pull me to him hard and fast without saying a word.

Like one night, it was storming so bad I stayed over. Tuck told me if Emmylou had been a boy he was going to name her Buffalo; his brown buffalo hat was right there next to him on the couch and I picked it up, put it on my head. He asked me my favorite Dwight Yoakam song. I said "Fast as You" so easy like it was my middle name because for me there ain't no other Dwight Yoakam song. Told him it was sexy, lonesome. And Tucker started playing it right there for me and singing the chorus and he was singing it like Dwight. I covered my hot face with my hands. I didn't get paid to think about Tucker putting that guitar down and slowly slipping his tongue into my mouth and taking off his gray sweatpants, but I was thinking about it anyway. I wanted to feel how Thelma felt about J.D. in *Thelma & Louise,* minus the awful parts. Just that part where she goes to the diner the morning after and gets all wide-mouth laughing at Louise before hell breaks loose again. When she pulls her collar out and points at the hickey on her neck — that part, jittering on the VHS screen of my heart.

So I was walking in front of Tucker, swaying my hips, but not too much. That turquoise feather skirt looking like the sun had lit it up, the blue holding the bright. Tuck was singing under his breath and we were almost to the elevator. He was slow poking, taking his time like he always did.

"I see you up there looking beautiful," he said with his scritch-scratch voice from so much singing and growling under rising summer moons night after night, all over. He said it kind of low. Kind of like I wouldn't hear him, but I did. I was listening with every part of my body. Hoping he'd leave Shay. Feeling the weight of the wait. The carmine-hot wanting. I would've heard him if he hadn't said a word.

We were fixing to get on the elevators and I didn't even turn around. I was thinking I could be as fast as he was — knowing someday Tuck'd write a song about this. Knowing I'd finally planted a seed back there somewhere and now all I had to do was sun it and water it and be as patient as patient could be. I looked down at Emmylou and said, "Say thank you, Daddy." Then I said it too, like a good girl. Kind of slow. Meant it.

Thank you, Daddy.

CHATEAU MARMONT, CHAMPAGNE, CHANEL

He is no mystery to me, *we* are no mystery to *us*. He travels, I travel, *we* travel but not always together. When I am home alone, he writes to me: *Miss K. Huff, traveling.* Stiff, washy office-blue envelopes, perfect squares. Typewritten letters on expensive paper, gentle-sweetly barking at me in all caps spaced cleanly down the middle of the page. This time it reads:

CHATEAU MARMONT, CHAMPAGNE,
CHANEL UPCOMING FRIDAY
BEFORE DINNER UNTIL SUNDAY
AFTER BREAKFAST

X
M

And that's what I always call him, *M.* Spoken aloud, written down, zip-whispered in little blue electric bursts from my beeping phone to his vibrating one. I send him a text on a Tuesday.

Dear M, I will be there.

Promise?

Have I ever lied to you?

No. I don't think so? Maybe?

No!

I pack my moisturizer and tingle-foaming face wash, toothbrush and toothpaste. A thin dress and two pairs of white lace panties. A long, light sweater and two pairs of leggings. A white triangle bikini. My hard pink suitcase. I put my big, clear-plastic sunglasses on my face like two black eye-moons. My little bottle of allergy pills rattles around, making music in my purse with my lipglosses. I pack a book, although last time I packed a book I didn't take it out of my bag. It is the same snaky Joan Didion I always take to California, but never read.

M is already there, hogging a whole couch to himself. M is already there, hogging California to himself. M is already there because M is always early, never late and M is particular, but not impatient. M is my James Bond in his pressed white dress shirt and slim blue tie, with his flat-front navy pant legs crossed, the thin-striped socks I'd given him, slipping into one acorn-colored cap-toe Oxford shoe resting upon his knee, the other flat and still on the floor. A sculpture. M is reading the newspaper like it is the sixties or seventies or eighties or nineties. M has gifted me diamond earring chunks the size of thumbtacks and I am wearing them for him. I wear everything for him. Cool touches of perfume on my neck and my wrists and the backs of my knees. A breezy white dress with pockets, white Birkenstocks. I've painted my toenails the softest pink I could find. A whisper. I sit close to him so our thighs touch and he puts his arm around me.

"We were here only three months ago?" he asks after saying hello and kissing my mouth.

"Yes," I say.

"You look smashing."

"Thank you."

"Where were we last month?" he asks. He sniffs my neck.

"Mountains," I hint.

"Ah, mountains," he says, before standing and offering me his arm. He bends to get my suitcase. "Drinks in the room?"

"Chateau Marmont, champagne, Chanel," I say, nodding.

"Chateau Marmont and Chanel," he says, looking around. He takes my wrist, turns it over and puts his nose there.

"Champagne," I say, wanting.

I slip off my sandals, leave them by the door. He sits on the edge of the bed and unties his shoes. His brown leather bag has beat us to the room. We order in the charcuterie, a smoked trout salad, an aged strip steak bourguignonne and fries, the prime filet mignon with oregano butter and asparagus. But before we eat! Glitter in a glass, the ice of his peppermint breath.

"Isn't it so pretty how they say a *flight* of wines?" I ask him when we are full. I am bubble-drunk, sitting cross-legged on the bed next to him, knowing full-well he can see my panties. He's taken his shirt and tie off so he won't stain them, his pants too. Hungrily, I watched him loosen his tie. I love watching him loosen his tie. Now he is in his white undershirt and underwear and I am still in my white dress, boldly brave enough to eat and drink everything without fear of ruining it because I know he loves that about me. My defiance — and arousing. To me. To him.

"*Who* says flight of wines?" he asks.

"The wine-tasting people," I say. I flip through a glossy, heavenly-smelling magazine I've found in the bedside table drawer.

89

"It's lovely. Them saying that," he says.

"Did someone die in this room? Someone famous?" I say.

"John Belushi died in Bungalow 3."

"And Jim Morrison used to live here," I whisper, as if Jim is one room over and I don't want him to hear me.

"It's earthquake-proof."

"*And* haunted."

The condensation of sadness that presses against us — leaving us damp and cool — fills the room at the word *haunted*.

"Let's not die here."

"No, let's not die here," I repeat. *We have plenty of time to die,* I don't say.

"We don't talk about death in California," he warns himself gently. Contrite. His attempt at fanning away the grief-smoke that chokes us, stains the glass of our shattered hearts.

We make quiet love and go to the pool.

We go to the pool and come back. The bed, again.

M bosses me around.

Kiss me. Fuck me. Harder. Pull your hair back. Touch yourself. Beg me. Call me Daddy. Suck it. Spread your legs. Wider.

M is shirtless, in white pajama bottoms. We've gone out to the hills, watched the sunset. The jacaranda as God-purple as the sky, the sky as God-purple as the jacaranda. Our California is outrageously dry and lousy with flowers.

Our room again: I've brushed my teeth, but am drinking more champagne anyway. M is sitting by the wide-open balcony doors, smoking a cigarette with his legs stretched out. The wind and the curtains, ghosting. He is the only man I've loved like this. *Have you ever loved anyone else?* He has asked me plenty of times when he is inside me, his mouth pressed against mine. My forever-answer: *No, M; not like this.*

I watch him smoke with his no-wedding-ring left hand. M is quiet. M was quiet *before,* but he's even quieter now. M is contemplative, cerebral. M is terrible at arguing. Early in our relationship, M used to think we were breaking up any and every time we argued. Some things we argued about back then: Me, feeling emotionally abandoned. Him, feeling emotionally abandoned. Me, jealous of the time he was spending with other people. Him, jealous of the time I was spending with other people. Me, worried he was opening up to someone else who wasn't me. Him, worried I was opening up to someone else who wasn't him. Me, annoyed when he was too quiet. Him, annoyed when I talked too much.

M used to think our fights meant no more hotels. No more room service. No more champagne on the starlit balcony. No more sharing a cigarette after sex. No more sharing an apple after a nap (specifically, no more of him holding the cold, sweet crisp to my mouth and letting me bite and him making sure to put his mouth in the exact spot where mine was). No more matching white robes after baths. No more of him rubbing coconut oil on my feet after our showers. No more of his bearded face disappearing between my legs (also, no more of me getting on my knees in front of him). No more sharing minty space in front of the mirror. No more Sinatra Sunday mornings, Nina Simone nights. It took him years to understand how I could fight with him and get over it. That our fights never meant I loved him less. I watch him smoke and think of this: *M, I love you and nothing and no one can ever stop me.*

"What are you thinking about?" he asks without turning around. His voice — a warm, gray wool net casting out into the California night, catching those California stars that would zoom-power-up and shoot out from his eyes if only he would turn to me. His arm, thrown over the back of the chair like a slack rope.

"We are far from home," I say.

"Does that bother you?" he asks. He smokes.

A trumpet somewhere below us. Barely, but I can hear it! And do you know what else I can hear? The nightswimmers — tender splishes echoing off the white-weathered concrete and blackness. I am wet-haired in my robe on the bed and more in love with M now than I've ever been. Like kudzu, devouring me. Like a gremlin I fed after midnight.

"No. I like how we got here," I say.

I am waiting for M to turn and look at me. *Please look at me. Look at me.*

"Next month we'll meet somewhere different, but California keeps us," he says over the pale brown moon of his shoulder.

California, keep us, I pray in Jesus' holy name.

93

BEARISH

My husband's granddaddy felled the bear upon the rangy earth of Wyoming — the grassy compass back of that American square, a spread-wide book of glory. I flirt with Granddaddy for the memory, the bearskin rug. I tap the bear's teeth and feel my fingernails echo. I stare into its nothing glassy-black eyes. I give the bear a Scottish accent. I am listening to an audiobook read by a man with a Scottish accent; the cadence of his voice is fuzzy paper crumpling and crumpling and smoothing out again. I take the rug home and lose my clothes, crawl naked under the hairy heft of it. Imagine the Scottish accent saying I am a bear too. *You are. A female bear is called a sow. A group of bears is called a sleuth.* I wait — stilly as the dead bear's heart — for my husband to come home from work. When he finds me, I growl. I grunt and howl like Tom Waits. He loves Tom Waits. My husband pets the stiff black hair on the bear's head. This is making up. *You have a devastating personality, Dolly. Absolutely crushing,* he says to me, deepening his dimples. I rise like the moon and open my slick strawberry mouth.

ALL THAT SMOKE
HOWLING BLUE

The first thing Bo ever said to me was that I had a face like an alarm clock — resplendent enough to wake him up. He and his younger brother, Cash, ran a garage on the shitty side of town. My car was always busted. That's how we met.

Since then, I'd been living with both of them — driving Bo's old truck whenever I wanted and kissing Cash when Bo was at work. Bo knew about the kissing, I just didn't do it in front of him. I slept in Bo's bed most nights unless he really pissed me off. I loved them both equally. I used to make a peanut butter and jelly joke about it, but no one understood what I meant. Bo kept his shoulder-length hair slicked back and Cash kept his short. See? They were different.

Bo had been teaching the blue-eyed shepherd puppy to howl and that's what they were both doing — sitting on the floor, howling at the ceiling. Bo was picking leftover bits of tobacco from his tongue and I reminded him again that he shouldn't smoke in the house. My hair was scented with woodsmoke from the fire we made out back the night before. Bo stood and put his nose on my neck and sniffed me real good. I was at the stove stirring the baked beans.

"Mercy," he said. Soft. It was the name my mama had given me and he said it a lot. It made me feel special how it got both meanings coming from his mouth. My name, a begging blue prayer. We kissed. Bo's kisses were feathery, Christmas-sweet. Cash hungry-kissed like a soldier on leave.

Bo stuck the puppy underneath his arm and stepped outside. I watched the puppy through the screen, howling up at the sky. The puppy was licking Bo's face.

Cash came through the front door and gently kicked my boots aside to make a path.

"I thought it was my night to make dinner," he said, clinking a six-pack on the kitchen counter.

"You can tomorrow. I made fried chicken, potatoes and baked beans. Biscuits are in the oven. I got Bo to open the can since it scares me so bad when it pops," I said.

"Well, at least he's good for something, right?" Cash said, barely laughing.

"He's out back teaching the puppy to be an asshole," I said, pointing with the wooden spoon, careful not to drip.

"Will you cut my hair tonight?" Cash asked, taking off his ball cap and opening a beer.

"Why? You got a crush on some girl you want to look cute for?" I asked.

"Yep. Some girl named Mercy," he said, smiling. I twinkled.

The sunset light ached at the windows. The puppy let out a brushy itty-bitty howl that went on forever. It kept right on crackling. I'm telling you, I thought it'd never stop.

PINK BUBBLEGUM
AND FLOWERS

Sweet-sticky pink bubblegum in my mouth, blowing bubbles. Bored, peeking on the guys Dad paid to come over to rebuild the deck. My little brothers were in the living room playing some video game that made it sound like a spaceship was hovering over our house, waiting. I was home one more week for the summer before I went back to college four hours away. I had friends, close girlfriends, but none of them were around. Bored, peeking on the one guy especially. The youngest-looking one, maybe he was twenty-one. Barely. I put on eyeliner and shiny red lipgloss, went out there and asked if they needed anything.

The guy in charge, the one with the beard and mirrored sunglasses, the pencil behind his ear, introduced himself to me. Gary Something. There were four of them. Gary Something and Trevor No Last Name and Pete No Last Name and the only one I cared about was Jordan. Helloooo, Jordan. Jordan looked like he belonged in a movie about the young guy who comes to work on the housewife's house when the husband is away and Jordan ends up having sex with the housewife in the kitchen while the teapot screams and sizzle-boils over. Jordan was sweaty and shirtless. He literally glistened. I was obsessed with Jordan. That quick. It only took an hour. I hadn't been obsessed with anyone since Rafael and that was a couple months ago. He texted me sometimes but bored bored bored.

I'd texted him that earlier in the day.

bored bored bord

I didn't even apologize for the misspelling. He never wrote me back.

Jordan slipped his shirt on as he walked over to me. Sad face.

"Hi. Sorry. Hope we're not being too loud," he said.

I didn't know anything about Jordan except:

He had a white truck.

He had a white shirt.

He had jeans and boots. Probably socks, too.

His name was Jordan.

He worked with these other dudes.

His water bottle was blue.

He had some tools. Or someone let him use their tools.

I stood there looking at him, annoyed at myself for still having that wad of gum in my mouth. It was giving me a headache and it wasn't even sweet anymore. I took it out and tossed it in the trash bag the guys were using.

"Yeah, my dad said it would be loud. The hammering and sawing or whatever. Annoying," I said. I wasn't really annoyed, but I wanted Jordan to think I was. I wanted him to think I hated him for at least a split second.

"My bad. I mean, it kind of *has* to be loud. Circular saws are loud. That's what they do."

"Wow, mansplaining saws *and* sounds to me?" I said.

"Damn. Sorry," he said, smiling and laughing like we were old buds.

I gave him a thumbs-down.

He gave me a thumbs-up. I finally smiled at him, but only barely.

"So, yes or no. Did y'all need anything?" I asked them. I looked around Jordan at the other guys.

"No thanks! We'll let you know," Gary Something said. Gary was probably Jordan's dad. He looked enough like Jordan.

Jordan took his shirt off again. He'd only put it on to talk to me.

I went inside.

My brothers were still playing their video game. They were old enough to make their own lunch, but I asked them what they wanted since I was in the kitchen anyway. I could see the guys working on the deck from the kitchen window. I would sneak and look when I was sure they couldn't see me. I didn't want Jordan to see me watching him. I didn't know the guy and he could be a serial killer, a rapist, one of those guys who dragged women back to his cave by their hair.

"Pizza or mac and cheese, little turds?" I asked my brothers, turning my back to the sink. I imagined Jordan catching a glimpse of my shoulders, the straight-up rock bone stacks of my spine.

"Pizza!" Angel said.

"Mac and cheese!" Aidan said.

"Not both! One!" I said, stepping into the living room. I imagined Jordan leaning over, pressing his hot mouth to the kitchen window glass before I walked away, catching a glimpse of my twenty-year-old apple ass.

"Chloe, move!" Angel said, fanning his

arm from side to side. I was standing in front of the TV.

"Put the mac and cheese *on* the pizza please," Aidan said. He was the peacekeeper, the most rational one.

"Fine," I said.

I put a frozen pizza into the oven and put a pot of water for mac and cheese on the stove. While I waited, I went through the messages on my phone. Rafael had texted me back.

Hey. Wyd?

making mac and cheese pizza for my brothers

You still bored?

there's this hot guy working on my deck

So . . . you're not bored anymore?

idk why?

I could come over?

you're in town?

For a little bit.

ok sure

See you in like 20 mins.

The water was close to bubbling and I put the noodles in. I told the boys to listen for the pizza timer. I told them I was taking a quick shower. I told them Rafael was coming over. They nodded and kept playing their game. I told them to pause it.

"If you don't take the pizza out when the timer goes off, it'll burn. You understand what I'm saying? I don't trust you two," I said, stabbing at them with two fingers.

"Chloe, we're ten and twelve. Not two," Angel said.

"Then act like it," I said, flipping them off.

Angel flashed his middle finger at me.

"Okay," Aidan said, before unpausing the game.

I showered, washed *and* conditioned my hair using my mom's expensive shampoo and Chanel body wash. I thought about Rafael putting his hands on me. I thought about Jordan putting his hands on me. I thought about Rafael and Jordan putting their hands on me at the same time. I was so thankful I didn't see smoke or smell anything burning when I walked out of the bathroom, the shower steam following me like a little Winnie-the-Pooh rain cloud. I smelled so good. I pressed my nose to my wrists and breathed in in in in in.

I would keep my hair up in a towel until Rafael got there. I wanted him to know I took a shower because he was coming over. I wanted Jordan to maybe see me too. I didn't care about the other guys working on the deck. The boys had followed my directions with the pizza and the pasta for the mac and cheese was done. I put on clothes, left my hair up, drained the pasta, squeezed the packet of cheesy sauce over it, and told my brothers to come and get it. My house was full of and surrounded by boys, there was a boy coming over. I needed to text my mom, I needed to talk to a woman.

i need to bleed. it's time to start my period. i'm so cranky.

You're not pregnant? LOL right? ;)

mama no! IMPOSSIBLE RIGHT NOW. are y'all having a good time?

My parents were on a Love Weekend in Cincinnati. That's what they called it. Every year, they went away for two days at the end of summer.

Yes we are. The deck guys are doing fine? No creeps?

My mom always liked to ask *no creeps* whenever I was around any men.

no creeps. they're nice. one's cute.

LOL. Text or call anytime you need to. The boys ok?

the boys are fine. i made them mac and cheese pizza.

You're a sweet sister. Love y'all.

love y'all too.

I didn't tell her Rafael was coming over

105

because I didn't know what it meant yet. I didn't know what it meant when Rafael showed up at the front door either. I stepped out on the porch as I held the door open for him and saw Jordan going into the back of his truck for something. He looked up at me. I made quick eye contact with him before I went back inside.

"So, what are they doing?" Rafael asked, leaning toward the kitchen sink to get a better look out of the window. He did this after he'd said hey to my brothers and talked to them about the video game. He'd said he'd gotten it recently too. Apparently every dude in the world was obsessed with this video game and guys always tried to make it seem like girls were the silly ones. Annoying.

"Building a new deck," I said, like it was the most obvious thing.

"Is that you?" Rafael asked, turning toward me.

"Is that me, what?"

"That smells like pink bubblegum and flowers?" He leaned forward and put his nose on my neck, inhaled.

I giggled a little and took my hair down from the towel.

"I guess," I said, heading toward the hallway, the bathroom. Rafael followed me.

I met Rafael at college but Rafael and I were from the same town. We didn't know it until we got to college. Rafael had half dated a girl on my floor I didn't know and she gave me the stink eye when Rafael started coming to my room instead of hers. She felt like she owned him and I did too. Something about Rafael made me feel like he belonged to me and *only* me, even though he was never my boyfriend. We'd never had full-on sex. He'd gone down on me once after a party and one other time I gave him a blowjob in his car. I liked thinking about both those nights a week apart, before the spring weather showed up. We'd been together in our own way from around Christmas until after Valentine's Day when he gave me some roses and a bottle of champagne and gave the same gift to another girl too. I knew because she told me and even though I "broke up" with him because I was embarrassed about it, I stayed obsessed with him and we kissed at parties sometimes, but never went any further than that again. He never told me to stop texting him or to leave him alone. Even when I'd text him late at night, even when I'd write him boring texts about how bored I was or how I didn't have very many friends left in town anymore. How I was working at the coffee shop up the road, but didn't want to be a barista every summer. He didn't want to be anyone's boyfriend, but in a way he was *everyone's* boyfriend because he never told girls no. Rafael was a yes-man.

His mother was black and Puerto Rican, his dad was some country white dude. Rafael had this beautiful black hair that could swoop down over his eye like a feather, like a God-touched thing. He wore skinny gray pants and his thin patterned shirts unbuttoned. His style waffled between rock star and just crawled out of a dumpster after a long night of drinking, but he made it work. And I liked them both.

"You smell *so* good," Rafael said, leaning against the frame of the bathroom door.

I was putting my leave-in conditioner in my hair and the bathroom was still heavy with Chanel and pink. I was a deep, thick, fecund garden. Rafael had his nose up in the air, sniffing like a dog.

"I didn't know you were coming back home," I said, knowing how bad he wanted me, because I wanted him that bad too. I thought of Jordan out back and what he wondered about Rafael and me here in the house. If he imagined Rafael touching me in here. Even if Jordan was like the best guy ever he would think about it for at least a second. It wasn't even all that pervy. It wasn't like I was underage. He wouldn't have to be a creep or anything.

Rafa met my eyes in the mirror. That's what the girls called him sometimes. *Rafa.* I'd heard his buddies call him that too. And maybe his brothers. He had two brothers, like me. I'd met them both when they came to pick him up at school for Christmas. I watched them load up his brother's car from my dorm room window. Watched Rafa tie his hair back with a red bandanna and share a can of beer with his little brother before they took off and tossed it in the recycling bin by the front door. He was responsible, how hot. Most guys would've tossed the can on the ground or in the trash. Rafa was a recycling hero.

"Do you want to know why I came back home?" he asked.

"Do you *want* to tell me why you came back home?" I asked, scrunching my wet curls with my slippery fingers.

"I had to testify against my dad for . . . hurting my mom. Me . . . and my brothers had to," he said. Softly. He wasn't looking at me in the mirror anymore, he was looking down. I gasped and turned around.

"What?!"

Rafa pressed his index finger against the wood of the door frame like he was purposely leaving evidence for someone to find later. *Rafa was here.*

"It smells *exactly* like pink bubblegum and flowers in here. It's like . . . calming me down," he said. And as soon as he said it, my brothers whooped and hollered from the living room. I heard one of them go into the kitchen, open the fridge, close it again. Someone out back turned on the circular saw, but not for long. They hammered and hammered and hammered. They were listening to Tom Petty and I could hear it too. *Wildflowers.* I loved that album, that song. It reminded me of my dad and being a little girl. Rafa was right. The smell *was* so calming and Petty's voice was gentle and calming, too.

But! We were talking about something awful and when I remembered, my legs got kind of wobbly and hot.

"Are you okay?" I asked. I didn't know how many people he'd told about this. I didn't know how many other *girls* he'd told about this. I hoped none. I hoped he was telling me first and telling me only. I wanted this to be something we shared, something we bonded over. His secrets were better than sex.

Rafa met my eyes again and it felt like we were alone in the house together. Like everyone else had been raptured up. The heat, the perfume, the steam, all of it — hypnotizing us. I gently tugged on his shirt so he'd come all the way into the bathroom and I closed the door. The Tom Petty seemed to get louder and my eyes were tearing up. My hair was cold on my neck. I sat on the lid of the toilet. Rafa sat on the floor with his back against the door and told me everything.

He told me his parents were going through a catastrophically messy divorce and how his dad hadn't been violent with his mom or him and his brothers growing up, but in the last couple years he seemed to lose . . . *something.* Or gain . . . *something.* Rafa didn't know which one it was. And when Rafa was home for spring break his mom and dad got in a huge fight and his dad grabbed his mom's arm and he slapped her hard across the face. His mom called the police and Rafa and his brothers jumped on his dad and beat him up. The cops who came knew his mom well from working security at the grocery store where she was manager and the cops wouldn't press charges against Rafa or his brothers. They threw his dad in jail. And the cops needed Rafa and his brothers to come down and make some more statements about what happened that night, so Rafa and his brothers did it. His dad was going to have to do some real jail time. Like, six months or maybe even a year. Which didn't seem like enough to me after hearing Rafa describe it, after seeing Rafa's face as he told the story.

He didn't cry, telling me, but I kind of wanted him to. I'd never known him to be overly emotional and wanted a peek. I felt dirty for it, using some tragic thing that was hurting him in an attempt to get to know him better, but he trusted me enough to tell me, to come over, to tell me everything. The Tom Petty, the hammering, the heaven-smelling bathroom and the intimacy of Rafa sharing his secrets with me — all of that sounded and smelled and felt like something important enough to let in. To remember. To file away for later, when I needed it. Like a first-aid kit or something, just in case.

I went to Rafa and sat in his lap, kissed him, let him pet my hair like I was a cat.

"It does smell really good in here," I said.

"It does," he said.

Rafa hung out for a while, even played a round with my brothers. Afterward, I told the boys it was time to take a video game break and they disappeared outside with their shorts and ratty sneakers and their friends from next door and across the street and down the street. I told them to be back in like, two hours. I told them to remember to take their water bottles. I told them to be careful.

Rafa and I usually had crackly-electric sexual tension, but now it was kind of sad too because of the stuff with his mom and dad and because we weren't in the bathroom anymore. The powerful pleasant smell had gone away, but the perfume was in my hair, on my wrists. We were sitting in the living room, staring at the TV, neither of us paying too much attention. He finally kissed me and I was relieved. The guys out back were working and listening to music and Rafa and I were on the couch, not even hot-and-heavy making out, but kissing and being close and quiet together. Everything was quiet and peaceful and good-smelling inside, but it got loud out front as the guys started loading up their things. The *clang-*

slip of metal, the *clap-smack* of wood. I heard a woman's voice too. I was jealous; it was probably Jordan's girlfriend and there I was jealous of Jordan's girlfriend while I was underneath Rafa on the couch and I loved him. Probably.

I sat up and went to the window, looked out. There was a woman, standing with the deck guys. Jordan seemed to be ignoring her. That made me feel better. She was talking to the Mark one. No, there wasn't a Mark one, right? Pete. She was talking to Pete. The other guys were getting in their trucks, ready to leave and Jordan was leaning against his.

"What's up?" Rafa asked me.

"I don't know. Some woman is out here talking to the deck dudes," I said and quickly realized they were arguing. Jordan was looking at his phone and Pete and the woman were cursing at one another and she was pointing in his face. He moved her hand away.

Rafa stood and came to the window to look out with me. Jordan wasn't turning around, wasn't paying any attention to Pete and the woman fighting. How did she find our house? Did he ask her to come over? As soon as I knew the deal, I'd text my parents about it because whatever was happening was way weird.

The woman put her hand in Pete's face again and this time he hit her hand and swatted it away.

Rafa took a deep breath in and let out a groan. He went over to the door, snatched it open.

"Don't put your hands on a woman like that," Rafa said. Loud. My blood jumped. I asked what was going on.

"Nothing," Pete snapped.

Jordan put his phone away and held both hands up.

"This is what they do. We'll leave. We were just leaving," he said.

"Don't touch her," Rafa said, walking toward them.

"It's his wife," Jordan said at *exactly* the same time Pete said, "It's my wife."

"I don't care. You put your hands on her in front of me, you may as well put your hands on me. Piece of shit," Rafa said, standing right in front of them.

"Rafael. Don't," I said. I didn't want him getting beat up! I didn't want him getting in a fight at all! Everything had been so perfect and good-smelling before and now everything was turning awful! A sudden drop in pressure, everything upside down.

"Get the hell out of here." Pete made a

dismissive swipe with his hand and the woman stepped away. All I saw was Rafa's black hair jump forward and back like a fussy-winged fruit bat taking flight as he punched Pete in the face. Jordan grabbed Rafa's arms in an instant, held them behind his back. The boys were sweaty and breathing hard and smashed together and it should've been kind of hot, but I was annoyed and freaked out. The woman sat in the grass by the driveway and put her face in her hands. I jumped off the porch to be closer to them, but not too close. I was scared to get in the middle of it. I went to the woman and asked if she was okay and she said yes.

"Why can't men ever calm the fuck down?!" I said to her. She laughed a little. I put my hand on her shoulder. "Rafa! Stop!" I said. Loud. We were being so damn common and country in the front yard with the trucks and the fighting and the hollering, like none of us had any home training.

Pete held his fingers to his bleeding lip and said who are you to Rafa. Pete looked like his feelings got hurt more than his face.

"We're leaving," Jordan said to me, holding Rafa's arms. And it was sweet how he said it. Like, he knew it was what I wanted. "Pete, let's get out of here," he said, still not letting Rafa go.

"He's my boyfriend," I said to them about Rafa. I said it to Rafa too. This was a perfect time to show off and it felt good with the sun lighting us up. I felt bad for the woman and I didn't want Pete treating her like that. Maybe I could be a decent distraction from it?

Rafa softened his eyes and smiled.

"You're so damn beautiful. You smell so good," he said. "Te amo," he said to me right there for the first time. Right there with Pete holding an old white, dirty T-shirt to his bloody, busted lip and Jordan holding Rafa's arms and Pete's wife breaking sticks at my feet.

"Aw, I love you too. Te amo," I said with the top of my head warming up with passion and adrenaline and the summer heat. I smelled the inside of my wrist. I smelled so good. I stepped closer to Rafa so he could smell me too. Held out my wrist so he could take a big sniff and a bee zip-buzzed right onto my bare shoulder like I was a flower.

Knock Out the Heart Lights So We Can Glow

Exie roamed the aisles of the twenty-four-hour grocery store when she got lonely — touching things and gently placing cans and paper cartons in her little basket, only to make a loop and put them back on the shelves. She liked the music they played. Songs about trusting Jesus and boys driving around with girls and first kisses on front porches. She was drawn to the dusty items no one else seemed to love. A long, crinkly-packaged stripy jump rope on a crooked rack in the cereal aisle. Weird, local home-made sauces in the condiment aisle. Her favorite jar was *Eula's Egg Sauce.* The drawing of Eula was sweet-smiley and big-busted. Exie had never met either of her grandmothers, but she liked to think that they were like Eula. She bought the sauce and went to her car. Locked the doors, opened the jar, stuck her tongue in and licked. The sauce was goopy pudding-thick and yellow, but Exie thought it tasted purple. At home, her husband, in his sleepiest blanket-voice, asked her where she'd been. "Do you remember when I was eating pineapple and started to cry because I was alive and some people weren't?" she asked. Reminded him of that morning after church when her hair was baptism-wet. How she sat at the kitchen table, born again, drowning in the sunlight. Her husband was a good man and she loved him, but he didn't know how to be special, how to glow. She said it was pretty simple and she'd teach him. There was no big secret. You just had to let the things in your heart get real dark first.

GET ROWDY

I told every one of those guys I could do some things to make them forget how much Rowdy owed them. As long as they promised not to kill Rowdy or put him in the hospital. They had to leave him alone for good. I gave them all the same speech, every time.

"I know he's a fuck-up. Trust me. I've known him since high school. Our daddies used to work together up until his daddy died in his sleep couple years back. Everybody knows he's no good. I'm just trying to help him out."

Rowdy's daddy's soul had slipped right out of his body real easy, like oil; Rowdy had a hard time wiping that oil off his hands. You think it's gone but when you get your hands wet, you see it. Beading up, streaking off. We weren't exactly together and we hadn't had sex yet and I didn't know why. Figured he might've looked at me like

I was a sister or something, but no. We kissed sometimes and made our dinners together. And sometimes I'd go over to his house in the middle of the night and climb into bed with him. We'd sleep.

I was in love with Rowdy and always had been. Big-time. I loved how he talked to me, how he said things. So plain. And I liked how most times he put his warm, rough hand on the back of my neck when he kissed me. He was no good, but I loved him anyway. He always had his gun, was always getting in fights down at the bar, always owed somebody money. We'd be at the bar and somebody would holler JACK and he wouldn't turn around. They'd holler JACK BOONE and he still wouldn't turn around. They'd say ROWDY because that's what everyone called him. And finally he'd tap some cigarette ash into an empty beer can, turn around and ask what the hell they wanted. That right there was what he was like.

One night, we wandered around under his neighborhood's sodium street lights, drinking beer, smacking creek cattails against the hot metal guardrails. When we got back to his place, Rowdy was half-drunk, half-asleep, and I asked him to tell me who he owed money to. He closed his eyes, mum-

121

bled them off. Six guys, six crazy names.

"Dallas, Hot Knife, Black Ray, Coot, Johnny Step, and Smoke," he said. I wrote them down, put question marks next to the ones I didn't know. I didn't want Rowdy knowing about it, so I had to ask around to find out who they were.

Easy. All I had to do was wear a low-cut shirt and ask the bartender if he knew a guy named Coot. Or Johnny Step. And if he didn't know, I asked the guys shooting pool and drinking by the back door. I only had to go to three different bars before I found some. Dallas and Black Ray were together.

"So, you're Rowdy's girl?" Black Ray asked.

"Not exactly," I said. Black Ray was pretty and tall, wore a big gold chain with a ship hanging from it.

"What'll you give me to leave him alone?" Dallas asked.

"How much does he owe you?" I asked.

I gave Dallas a quick, dry hand job in the bathroom. I had full-on sex with Black Ray in his car. Twice. He was sweet to me. Real sweet. It wasn't bad at all.

I scratched out their names.

~~Dallas~~, Hot Knife, ~~Black Ray~~, Coot, Johnny Step, Smoke

Went to Rowdy's place and climbed into

122

bed with him. He put his arm around me and I stared at the side of his face until my eyes got heavy and stayed closed. In the morning, I made him swear on the Bible he wouldn't get into any more trouble. He was superstitious and I told him my Bible had been blessed by a preacher I knew from New Orleans. Spooked him enough. He swore, kissed my hand. I followed him to work to make sure he was going where he said he was going and he did. I watched him climb up on the roof and start hammering in the wavy morning sun. Sat there watching him from my car and listened to the staccato beating of all those different tools echoing up the suburban sky. It was oddly dulcet and soothing.

Hot Knife looked like a California surfer, but he was from the Kentucky hills and sounded like it. Told me his real name was Danny even though I didn't ask. He had blond hair thick as rope and wore a leather motorcycle club vest over a white T-shirt. Told me Rowdy owed him nine hundred dollars.

"Danny, I don't have nine hundred dollars," I said, making a flirty-pouty face.

"How much *do* you have?"

I opened my purse, got my wallet out.

"I have seventy-five dollars. That's it," I said.

"You have pretty feet."

"Thank you." We both looked down at them.

He asked if he could paint my toes, so we went to the drugstore and he picked out a tropical orange bottle. I let him do a LOT of weird foot stuff and he told me to keep the seventy-five dollars. Also, he called me Theresa, but that isn't my name. It was fine. I didn't ask questions.

~~Dallas~~, ~~Hot Knife~~, ~~Black Ray~~, Coot, Johnny Step, Smoke

I made a habit out of following Rowdy to work every morning. I was taking a chance on him, believing he'd stop getting himself into crazy situations he couldn't get out of. I never caught him lying. I was the liar now.

Smoke worked at the tobacco shop. He said he'd seen me around a lot with Rowdy, told me Rowdy owed him some money. I gave him the speech, went down on him in the back office, and spit in the little garbage can next to the door on my way out — the slick black bag in there swished and caught the light.

~~Dallas~~, ~~Hot Knife~~, ~~Black Ray~~, Coot, Johnny Step, ~~Smoke~~

I found Johnny Step at the minor league

baseball game because it was dollar beer night and I heard he was always there on dollar beer night, never missed a game. He was shady and not nice and he scared me. I gave him the speech anyway, keeping my hand on the knife in my pocket the whole time.

"Let me get this straight. You're offering to *fuck* me so I'll leave that asshole alone?" he asked. He pointed at nothing and said it loud. My face got hot.

"Well, depends. How much does he owe you?" I asked.

He looked me up and down. Made a point of sizing up my ass. I took my hand off my knife, crossed my arms and gave him a look.

"About four hundred," he said.

His apartment was near the ballpark and when we went to his bedroom I turned around so I wouldn't have to look him in the face. He called me some awful names and it was the only thing that turned me on. And you know what? He might've acted the toughest, but he cried when he came.

~~Dallas~~, ~~Hot Knife~~, ~~Black Ray~~, Coot, ~~Johnny Step~~, ~~Smoke~~

Coot was hard to track down. He was out of town a lot and no one knew where, but I got lucky. Sat outside his house one night

125

and he came home to get a change of clothes.

After I gave him the speech he got a real sad look on his face, sat on the front steps.

"Did he put you up to this? I don't do business like that," he said.

"No, he didn't. I'm trying to help him out."

"He don't need your help. He needs to be a man," Coot said. He brushed some dirt off his boot.

"You're the last one on the list," I said. I thought I might cry, but I swallowed it, made myself all right.

"I'll tell you what. Fuck it. This is too sad. I don't want no part of it," he said, standing. He reached his hand down for me, pulled me up. He gave me a hug and it surprised me so much I couldn't help myself from crying. Coot held me and held me there against his chest, went into his pocket and handed me a piece of torn brown paper napkin.

"He ain't worth this, honey, I guarantee," he said.

"How much money does he owe you?" I asked, sniffing. I pulled back, wiped my nose.

"He ain't worth it," he said again, softly. Coot was old enough to be my daddy and I bet he would've been a good one.

~~Dallas, Hot Knife, Black Ray, Coot, Johnny Step, Smoke~~

My eyes were red from crying when I showed up at Rowdy's. He asked what was wrong. I told him nothing. PMS, girl stuff. The microwave beeped and he took out some leftovers from the night before when we'd cooked together and made baked spaghetti with fancy cheese on top. He pulled out the chair for me and asked if I wanted a glass of wine and I said yes. He'd just gotten out of the shower and smelled so good, like hotel soap and sunshine shampoo. I wanted to eat him up. His name was written in invisible ink on my list. I hadn't crossed it out yet but I wanted to. Bad.

"I've been thinking maybe we should talk about us. Like, moving in together or something. You're here all the damn time anyway and you know I love you, right?" Rowdy said, pouring wine and looking over at me.

"I love you too, Jack." My breath shivered out. I'd said *I love you, Jack,* over and over again in my diary when I was sixteen, my looping high-school-girl handwriting sprawling across those pale blue lines. I'd said it in my head when I went away to college and again when I flunked out and moved back home to our little town and saw him working on the roof next to my parents' house.

I got a nervous gut, letting those words out. I picked up my fork, crossed my legs underneath the table. He put the wineglass in front of me and sat down. I knew he might find out. I was sure one of those assholes would tell him what I did. But if he ever asked me I'd lie about it. That's what I was thinking as I sat there looking at Rowdy's smile. You should've seen it. That ignorant beautiful bastard's face lit up the whole room.

RE: LITTLE DOVES

We want him to. Make love. Kiss us. Touch us. All of us. He is our leader and we've chosen him; he is our leader and he's chosen us. Our love overwhelms and embarrasses us but we water it, grow it, nurture it and speak to it — this garden. We smoke hand-rolled cigarettes in a circle of succulents and rub sticky sagebrush and apricot mallow under our arms. We are safe and he does not hurt us. He is gentle and we can leave whenever we want. He tells us this. *You can leave whenever you want,* his breath bright with cumin and tea. His shirt and pants and beard and skin and hands scented with one of us, some of us, all of us. He calls us his little birds, his little doves. We do not call him God. He tells us this. *Don't call me God. I am not God. I am a man,* his breath sugar-heavy with blood-red wine and honey. He calls us his little animals, his little doves. We do not call him Daddy. He tells us this. *Don't call me Daddy. I am not your Daddy. I am your lover,* his breath blooming with cannabis and sandalwood. His shirt and pants and beard and skin and hands scented with myrrh and vetiver and bergamot and basil and lemon and patchouli. A soupçon of lust-musk. Little thunders of orange, bitter and sweet. We are grown women and we want him, need him. We are birds that can fly away and come back home; we are birds with a nest to tend. We are birds with babies to feed. His mouth to our mouth to their mouth. We are birds that can escape this but we don't want to. We want to be in the kitchen cooking for him, pregnant with seeds of him, watering them, growing them, nurturing them, speaking to them — our gardens. We wear sackcloth and pillowcase dresses and make dough with our rosemary hands. We put on our glowing nightslips and nightslip the bread into the oven, our fingers blued with berries. We close the kitchen windows to the Santa Anas — those devil winds — and we make sun tea on the back porch, waiting patiently for it, braiding each other's hair smoked with cedar and cinnamon. The hell-orange fires dragon-rage to the north. He lifts our dresses, his hands pinked with berries. He squeezes our thighs, our full bottoms, his hands warmed with kettle water. He drinks milk from our breasts, licks our nipples and sucks, climbs inside of us and we open wide. Our drowsy eyelashes sweep him away and back again — across the white dew of morning, the navy mist of night. We press our mouths against his, slip our tongues into his heat, brush our cheeks against his soft, dark, vanilla beard, against the tender buffalo plaid he pulls on when evening cools. We beg for this, we ache for this, we want this. He gives generously, unselfishly, not unlike a god. We moan and sing in our nest until we are sirens silenced. We smell of him until we bathe in lavender rainwater, in holy hyssop and serious moonlight — rapturously captive. He tells us, *You can leave whenever you want. Do you want to stay? Do you want this? Do you want? Do you? Say yes.*

OUT OF THE STRONG, SOMETHING SWEET

Always, the three of us. One black girl, two white girls in the sun — those clicky striped vinyl lawn chairs from 1985ish that Claire's dad still had in their garage for whatever reason. We were in the backyard, not the front. Last time we were out front, Mandy's asshole brother stopped in his red Stang and asked us if we knew what a pussy was before skeeing off and running the stop sign at the end of our street. Hannah had sat up and pushed her sunglasses atop her head. *Of course we know what a pussy is, asshole.* We were fourteen. Mandy's asshole brother was seventeen and thought he knew the world because his dad gave him that car. Because next year he'd be a senior. Like it mattered. What mattered is that he'd scared Claire and Claire had told her mom and Claire's mom had told Claire's dad and Claire's dad had walked over to Mandy's house and told Mandy's parents what her asshole brother had said to us. Claire's dad told Mandy's parents he'd better never catch her asshole brother ever talking to us again. Claire's dad could be scary. He always had a knife in his pocket, he rode a motorcycle, he looked like he'd done everything at least once. Claire's mom told us to lay out in the backyard instead. Never the front. So we did. And none of us were friends with Mandy anyway.

I wasn't trying to get tan the same way the white girls tried to get tan. How they'd hold their arms up to mine and say I'm almost as dark as you and I wouldn't say anything because everyone knows white people want to be black and no white person wants to be black. It's hard to understand because it's both. I liked how hot my skin could get out there. How good it felt to spritz water all over my arms and legs and lie there and smell like coconuts and think about boys and the stack of romance paperbacks I had waiting for me when I got back home. And Hannah and Claire and I actually liked each other, which my mom had told me was very rare, ever since the three of us met in elementary school.

My mom actually liked both of their moms too and my mom didn't really like

133

any of the other moms because she said they were the kind of women who grew up only wanting to be moms, they don't want anything else. "There's nothing else up here," she'd said, tapping the side of her head. When I grew up I wanted to be a mom like my mom and not like the other moms. Not like the moms with nothing else up there. I pictured empty rooms filled with empty cribs and empty milk bottles rolling against one another — a creepy, dirty mobile sputtering out a slow "Twinkle, Twinkle Little Star" on almost-dead batteries.

Hannah had a black boyfriend. Claire's boyfriend was from Mexico. I liked a white boy called Milo because his name was Milo. I didn't know where he was from. He was friends with their boyfriends. Our plan was to sneak out of Claire's bedroom window once her parents had gone to bed and meet the boys by the railroad tracks. We wanted to be out when the moon was full and high. Midnight. We weren't allowed to stay out past eleven. We'd been feeling dreamy all day, drunk on summer sun and tart strawberries and fizzy water. It was July and the day was dangerous; the words *twenty-second* made my mouth move like a kiss and a bite. Claire's house was big and her parents never woke up until morning. We'd showered and sat on her bed listening to music and watching the clock until it was time to leave.

Window open.

Climb out.

Reach back inside.

"Quiet."

"Be quiet."

"Seriously, shut UP."

Window closed.

"Where is Milo from?" Hannah asked quietly as we walked through Claire's neighbor's wet grass.

"Shh," Claire said.

"I'm whispering," Hannah snapped.

"It's not a question you need to know the answer to right this second. You can never chill," Claire said.

I laughed.

"Shh," Claire said again.

"Your shushing is louder than our laughing and whispering," Hannah said.

Claire laughed too. We were at the end of the street and finally Claire felt free. We all felt free. Somehow, her face was even frecklier by moonlight and I stood there looking at her, her purple hood pulled up, the little black-and-white shorts we passed between the three of us like an accidental *Sisterhood of the Traveling Black-and-White Shorts*. I loved Claire. I loved her so much. I loved Hannah too. I felt blessed by them and felt blessed to *know* it. I was one thing when I was alone. I was another, better thing when the three of us were together. We were walking quick, but I still prayed all lit up under the streetlight that we'd be friends forever. I was thinking *amen* when I heard Hannah's boyfriend *psst* us in the darkness. *Apsstmen.* We'd hung out so much, I even recognized his *psst.*

"Baby girl," Claire's boyfriend said. I saw him reach for Claire when we were in the light. I heard the chain fence rattle next to me. Milo's black hair, full moon-white skin. Hannah had already smashed herself into her boyfriend's arms.

"Hey," Milo said.

"Where are you from?" Hannah asked him immediately.

"Spearfish, South Dakota," he said.

"Who's from South Dakota?" Hannah asked, laughing.

"Me," he said plainly.

I decided I was in love with him.

He cupped his hand and lit his cigarette. His hair twitched across his face. I begged for mercy. He whipped his head back to adjust it. Mercy denied. I decided I would die for him — slit my neck and bleed out on top of him. Soak him like some Shake-spearean tragedy. You know, if he wanted me to. Like, for love.

"Come up here," Claire said from the train tracks stage. The moon, a spotlight.

We went up there and the boys talked about some other places we could go. They creeped us out talking about the Pope Lick Monster that haunted the railroad trestle bridge on the other side of town. Made people fall to their death.

"But that's not real," Hannah said.

"Trust me, it's real," her boyfriend said.

They started kissing. Claire's boyfriend asked her if she was scared of the monster and she said yes. Milo ignored them and told me he liked my watch. I pushed the little button on the side so he could see it light up. The blue of it, coloring the tip of his nose.

If we were feeling bold, but not bold enough to challenge the Pope Lick Monster, we could hop the next train. Maybe we'd make it and disappear. I'd start calling Milo *Moon* and I'd change my name too. I'd be *Dakota* so I could always remind him who he was, where he came from. He'd grow his black hair out and I'd braid it down his back, find a thin ribbon and tie it there. We'd get matching tattoos, some inside joke we hadn't even dreamt up yet, but when we got to the tattoo place it would come to us and the tattoo would always remind us of that night, that summer, that year, that specific gauzy feeling watering our eyes and warming our cheeks and numbing our tongues and tingling our faces when we were together.

If we were feeling violent, we could go to Mandy's house and beat the shit out of her asshole brother. Ask him if he knew what a pussy was. Take him to the bathroom mirror and tell him he was looking right at it. That's what a pussy was.

If we were feeling sad, we could sit in the rocky grass by the tracks and ask questions about God and why the world was the way it was. We could talk about evil. How it's inescapable and endless. How it's like death.

I could kiss Milo's neck or ask him to kiss mine. Have sex with him and get pregnant and be one of those moms I never wanted to be.

I could watch Hannah and Claire kiss their boyfriends and wish I had one. I could ask Hannah and Claire and their boyfriends if they wanted to kiss me. I could tell Milo I thought about him once in my bed. Under the covers. Okay, twice. Okay, three times.

Fine, every night.

I could do it. I could do anything. *We* could do anything. *Anyone* could do anything. We didn't need to escape *from* anything in order to escape. *Escape for escape's sake.* We could run and run and run and run and run. We could be running. We should always be running.

The train was coming when we saw Claire's dad walking toward us through the grass. The train was coming when I heard Hannah say shit and when Milo put out his second cigarette and kissed me on the mouth before hopping the fence. The boyfriends were running right behind him. Claire's dad didn't seem angry. His face was calm. He looked like an oil painting, the colors around him both bold and dark — the amber glow of the lamps lining the road, the pitchy midnight sky, his beaming white T-shirt and whatever color pajama pants. The orange tip of the cigarette he was smoking. That moon, that full moon, bewitching us. I even thought I saw him smiling. Or maybe it was the train making the lights flash his face. I was between the girls and we were holding hands. Claire was crying; Claire was always the first to cry. Her dad motioned for us to come toward him. His arm, a wing spread wide for us to hide under. We felt most like sisters with Claire's dad. He treated the three of us like a one-hearted girl. The boys were probably halfway across the neighborhood already; boys were always running. Claire said, Daddy. Hannah said shit again. Claire shushed Hannah and I resisted the urge to tell Claire it was too late to shush us. It didn't matter anymore. Claire's dad's mouth was moving, but I couldn't hear what he was saying. The train was too loud, too violent.

THE LENGTHS

Kieran was bottle green in her mouth —
the taste of wilted, salted kale. Sometimes
she convinced herself she could still hear
the popping Morse code braille of his tap
dancing, a kaleidoscopic map of sound leading the way back to him. Even when he was
home in Ireland. Even when he had shows
in New York. Even when he had shows in
New Zealand and she was in her American
bed alone with a steamy mug of tea and
clover honey, reading historical fiction about
dashing warriors thundering the ground on
leviathan, shadow-black horses.

They were a romance novel come to life,
only Kieran usually wore a too-big sweatshirt with the hood pulled up. God bless
the sexy superhero mysteriousness of a half-
covered face. He also danced on street
corners, in Irish pubs, restaurants, places
where people sat down for foamy black-
brown pints of Guinness, fried fish and

chips with thick wedges of lemon. Cottage pie, bangers and mash. Cheese and chive fritters, beef stew. Irish whiskey steak, soda bread, butter. Sticky toffee pudding.

The first time she saw him, someone at the table next to them said Kieran's quick feet cast a spell. Hypnotized. His legs, his muscular, wood-strong thighs — they were magic wands. Her friend snorted, she blushed. They Beavis and Butt-Head laughed.

Heh. Magic wand. Abraca-effing-dabra. Girrl, he can use his magic wand on me.

That first night, first kiss after the pub closed, Kieran handed her a frosty, pocket-sized bottle of bourbon. They passed it back and forth, draining it in the white winter night. The snow-pink sky was so pretty, it worried her. She ached. She could feel it in her back, the upper muscles of her arms.

What they became: muscle ache and massage, spoon and spoon rest. Relying on one another as much as snowflakes and Narnia lamppost light, helium balloon and string.

"Your hair, it's like . . . red clouds," she said, handing herself over to him — vanishing into the drumming of her bourbon-flickered blood.

Small And High Up

I.

Composing an email to him that I will not send: *William, I would save the buttons that come in those tiny plastic bags attached to your new dress shirts. Take pleasure in releasing the pins from the collar and turn it over to unpin the back, hearing the paper crinkle inside.* I want to tell William how much I love his ears. They are small and high up. I want to grab them and gently twist like I am opening a can of something. *I'd let you take me away from all this. Please. When I'm having an awful day, being in your presence lifts me like a little puff of air that keeps a feather from falling to the floor. I am embarrassed to tell you about the sadness I feel when I consider all the land in every city in every country in every world that is set aside to bury the dead. How the thought of it warms my face as if I've just opened the oven door. That heat — fervid, orange-pulsing and stealing breath.*

II.

I can see us in California, our future commune house and the farmhouse kitchen where I am soaking the rosemary garlic bread with extra-virgin olive oil. I gather the plum tomatoes we grow in our backyard, hammock them heavy in the hem of my sundress, staining the fabric with rainwater and dirt and rainwater and dirt and rainwater and dirt. I smell my hands before washing the tomatoes under the *hard-shh* flow of our kitchen sink. Before dropping them into the rolling, bubbling boil to soften and swell before I smash them between my fingers. William smells like cedar and peppermint, William smells like the Santa Anas. I won't care what anyone says, William will be my king and I will be his little bird. After dinner, I will tie my long hair back with a thick, slick ribbon. He and I will sit on the porch and drink and talk about how full we are. How we ate too much how could we eat that much why do we always do this. His black coffee, my ginger tea and lemon because I am pregnant with his lemon-sized baby and the ginger helps the nausea.

III.

William, let me tell you how I feel (small and high up!) when I look at your cuffed cerulean shirtsleeves, the expensive, slippery-silver watch sliding over your wrist bones. I wonder about alllll of your pale yellow bones and if your father ever fought in a war. I daydream about a time when you will make my entire body feel like an ear, like a fallen eyelash, a fingertip, pointing. I turn on my computer, open a blank email to him. Go stand in front of the refrigerator. Hold a full can of pop to my cheek, to the back of my neck. *William, you are so long. So tall. Like a monster, but not scary. I promise if you were my man, I'd let you make every part of me feel like a mouth. William, don't you want to make me feel like a mouth?*

SOME ARE DARK, SOME ARE LIGHT, SUMMER MELTS

You are scared of Nick, so you stall and tell him you have to stop by a friend's house. You tell Nick this friend is going to ride with you to drop Nick off at his place. The friend will sit in the backseat. You know how bad Nick's temper can be, so you say this gently, touch his shoulder when you tell him the friend is a guy. You've dated bad boys before, but Nick isn't a bad boy he's a bad *guy* and those are totally different things to you. You never meant for things to get this far. You should've gotten him out of your life the first time he grabbed your arm too hard. Or the second. Or the third. He doesn't grab your arm when you tell him your friend is a guy and he's going to ride with you. You are at a red light and you are staring straight ahead. You're a steel cage, careful not to cry.

The friend is Owen and you know Owen from the ice cream shop where you both work. Owen is kind without being flirty and maintains a boyish distance without being aloof. Owen's sweetness and genuine kindness is hard on people. It's almost stressful. How is he so great? Owen seems to be oblivious to how he makes girls feel, how he makes you feel comfortable and safe, like nothing could ever happen to you when he is around. When you and the other ice cream girls close up the shop at night, there are moments when you are anxious and afraid a man could show up. A brutal man, a man with a weapon, a man who would tie your hands and feet or put you in the freezer or rape you on the cold floor or kill you with a look. The ice cream girls are not anxious or afraid when Owen is there because he acts like he's never been scared of anything. He smiles before he goes outside to sit on the bench and read. Owen is casual about his phone use and sometimes he doesn't even take it with him. He sits there and reads. Actual books. Books like *On the Road* and the other Kerouacs. Kurt Vonnegut too. Once he was reading James Baldwin. Another time, a book of poems by Gwendolyn Brooks. He'd read "We Real Cool" to you as you stood there under the awning with him one day. He snapped his fingers and smiled at you, sweet. And when his shift was over he left without saying goodbye because he can do things like that without being rude.

You can trust Owen. And you are glad he answered your text.

Owen. Will you ride with me somewhere? I'll explain later. Can I come pick you up?

Yes. This sounds quite mysterious so how could I say no? I'm at home. Come on over.

Nick is pissed. Nick is always pissed. He's looking out his window. You have never told Nick about Owen and it's kismet that Nick has never been to the ice cream shop when Owen is there. Nick would've been immediately jealous because Owen is the kind of cute you like and Nick knows that. Nick is going to meet Owen soon and Nick will be even angrier than he is now. But this will fix it. Nick will leave you alone because something about Owen is magic. Nick doesn't have to know Owen is asexual. You would never tell Nick. Owen trusted you enough to tell you, so you trusted him back. Hard.

Owen is standing at the top of his long driveway. Nick shifts in the passenger seat and your anxiety instantly melts upon seeing Owen. He raises his hand at you before you stop the car. Owen sits in the back, the car filling with the smell of his house and whatever his parents made for dinner. Probably a hearty, healthy vegetable soup and a full glass of water.

"Hi," he says.

"Hi, Owen. Nick, this is my friend Owen," you say and smile, turning to Owen, but avoiding Nick's eyes.

"Nice to meet you, Nick," Owen says, touching Nick's shoulder. Nick nods. You let off the brake, gently press the gas pedal and begin the eleven-minute drive to Nick's place. Eleven minutes in the car with Nick and Owen. Eleven more minutes to be afraid of Nick in the passenger seat. Eleven minutes of conversation and music.

Nick mentions a street you have to turn down is under construction, so you'll have to go another way. Owen says he read about it on Twitter. You turn down the detour street, the sun gleaming off the street signs and the orange cones and the reflective vests of the construction workers. It's so bright you have to shield your eyes.

You flick to the oldies playlist and "Please Mr. Postman" comes on. The happiest song. So summery. Ice cream pop. You listen to the song at the ice cream shop. Owen mentions this.

"I know, right? It always reminds me of work," you say. Nick is looking out his window. "And ice cream."

"Ice cream tastes how 'Please Mr. Postman' sounds. It *sounds* pink," Owen says.

"It's a perfect song," you say.

"Absolutely, but it's too short. The really good songs like that are always shorter than three minutes and that's too short," Owen says. "It should be at *least* five minutes long."

Five more minutes, you think. You glance back at Owen and he smiles at you. Nick is still looking out the window and nothing about him feels pink. And when the minutes are finally up and Nick gets out of the car, he says to you call me later okay and you say okay even though you know you won't. You especially know you won't because Owen gets out of the backseat and opens the passenger door and sits in the seat and puts his foot down on the floor and steps on Nick's phone as you drive away.

"Oh. Nick accidentally left his phone," Owen says, holding it up for you. He holds it like it's his, a small intimacy. You feel a peach-soft tenderness toward Owen, even stronger than before because of it.

"Sweet. Let's go throw it in the river," you say, the thought sparking inside of you like lightning. *One Mississippi, two Mississippi.*

But you'll throw it into the mighty Ohio.

"Is that why you wanted me to ride with you? So we could go throw your boyfriend's phone in the river together?"

"He's not my boyfriend. Not anymore. And yes. Maybe. Maybe that is why," you say, giggling. The urge to cry has lifted and passed. The urge has gotten in the left lane and gunned past the same way you had gotten in the left lane and gunned past the two old women driving in front of you.

And once you make it to the river, Owen is the one who throws Nick's phone — skips it like a rock — across the wide, gray ribbon of water so you can't call Nick. Owen says you and him need to make a fat donation to a clean water fund, now that you've polluted the river with a phone. You agree.

"Are you worried Nick'll come to your house? Or come up to work?" he asks as you sit there.

"Kind of," you say. Shrug.

"Do you want to tell me exactly what he does to you?" Owen asks. And he sounds like a therapist, so you tell him that.

"My mom's a therapist," Owen says, nodding.

"Of course she is." You nod too. It explains so much about his listening skills, his ability to know when you need to talk.

"Do you want to tell me about it?" he asks. You do.

Nick gets angry over the tiniest things like you not replying to a text within two minutes and he stays mad about these things for days. Nick's emotional responses are disproportionate to the occasions. Once, Nick saw you say hello to a man you recognized from coming in the ice cream shop with his daughters and Nick was pissed all night about it. Kept asking who the guy was even though you kept telling him he was a guy from the ice cream shop who came in with his family. Everything makes Nick angry. Nick has issues. Nick comes from a crappy home and doesn't know better. Nick has to figure out his own life. Nick isn't awful all the time, you just didn't know how to break up with him without making him mad. That scared you, so you called Owen.

"Does he ever hurt you . . . physically?" Owen asks and looks right at you.

"He grabs my arm sometimes . . . when I turn away from him or when he wants to make sure I'm listening," you say.

"Show me," Owen says.

You put your hand on Owen's upper arm, squeeze and grab. Pull him closer to you.

"Not fucking cool," Owen says calmly like the weirdo he is, the weirdo who cares about

152

the environment and baby animals and how we treat one another. You feel bad about the rancid phone battery that will soon be polluting the river and mouth the word *sorry* up and out to the river, knowing it hears you, forgives you. Jesus does too. You smooth Owen's T-shirt back down, pat his warm skin. The sun ripple-winks on the river water like it should make a clink and it is raining in your heart. Pouring.

"Are you hungry? My mom made chicken tortilla soup. Do you want some chicken tortilla soup?" he asks.

"Yes," you say. And you get in your car and go full circle to Owen's place where Owen's mom is in the kitchen, loading the dishwasher. Owen's dad is out back, cutting the grass. You have never been inside Owen's place and now you're there, like leveling up in a video game. Owen has a friendly yellow dog that is tap-clicking around the kitchen floor like you are the greatest friend he's ever known.

"Mom, I was bragging to my friend from work about how good your chicken tortilla soup is and I figured it would be extraordinarily rude not to invite her over for a bowl, y'know . . . after all that bragging," Owen says. He tells her your name and there it is, sparkler-written across the air for a split second before it disappears.

"Absolutely! Nice to meet you. I'm Owen's mom," she says, offering her hand for you to shake. "And Malcolm's mom," she says as Owen's big brother bounds up the stairs from the basement.

Malcolm raises his hand in a wave and Owen tells you he'll be right back. The boys disappear down the hallway together. You are alone in the kitchen with Owen's mom who got one bowl down from the cabinet and is filling it with the soup on the stove.

"This is awkward, but thanks for feeding me. I feel like a stray dog. It's been a weird day," you say. You are not an orphaned child. You have two parents at home, a little sister, plenty of food. But being at Owen's feels like a kindness you didn't even know you needed.

"Pshh, it's not awkward. We're glad to have you. Do you have classes together too?" his mom asks, referring to the community college Owen goes to. You both graduated high school earlier that summer, but you aren't going to college. You are waiting. You don't know what you are waiting for.

"No, I'm sitting the fall semester out. I'm planning on going in the spring though," you say, not entirely sure if you're lying or not. You *have* thought about going in the spring, but you've done nothing more than think about it.

Owen's mom hands you your bowl of soup and a spoon, instructs you to sit at the kitchen table. Owen's dad's lawn mower in the backyard is far away from the house now, providing a distant buzzy hum. You can smell the grass and the smell of it makes you want to live forever in a place where summer never ends. You sit at the table and dig into your soup as if it's your kitchen, your mom at the coffeepot refilling before she sits across from you.

"So, a weird day?" his mom says.

"Yeah. Owen told me you were a therapist, so you're used to hearing pretty much everything, right?" you ask, swallow more soup. "This is the best chicken tortilla soup I've ever had, by the way. Thank you," you add. You especially like the lime because somehow, lime tastes like good luck.

"Pretty much heard it all, yes. And extra cocoa powder in the soup. That's my secret. I like your face, so I'll tell you," his mom says. You smile.

"Thank you. I like your face too," you say. Owen's mom belongs in a laundry detergent ad in her flowery, fitted button-down and slim jeans. Her hair is pulled up in a stylish

155

topknot and she is wearing a pair of reading glasses on a sparkly chain around her neck. She's really pretty and you wonder what Owen's dad looks like up close. You want to see which one Owen looks more like, because right now his mom is winning. Same nose and eyes. Same smile too.

"O said you were taking him on a mystery ride?"

You laugh a little and eat more soup, drink some of the water from the glass Owen's mom put on the table for you. You hear Owen and his brother down the hallway, talking excitedly about something and wonder if Owen will fill you in later or if it's a private thing, considering they are back there and not in the kitchen with you.

"I had a bad boyfriend and Owen made me feel better about it," you say.

"How did he make you feel better?"

"Just by being there, really," you say.

"Is everything okay now?" Owen's mom asks, leans forward with her hands holding her mug.

"Honestly, I don't know. But Owen made me feel better about it," you say again. You don't want to sound needy, but you don't mind letting Owen's mom know she's raised a good one. A gem.

"He's good at that," his mom says and

156

drinks her coffee.

"And that guy's not my boyfriend any-more . . . so," you say.

"Good. Owen talks about you. How well you two get along. You're far too pretty and interesting to have a bad boyfriend. Who needs that? Easier said than done, I know . . . but. If you *do* want to ever talk about it, you can talk to me," Owen's mom says and nods.

It makes you feel pathetic that Owen's mom feels like she needs to offer to lend an ear. You wonder what Owen has told her about you. If Owen feels sorry for you. Is this pity? Does pity feel like someone put-ting a warm coat over your cold shoulders? But it feels like Owen's mom is really *see-ing* you. The summer afternoon light slants through the window, lighting his mom up like some kind of angel. Or superhero. You picture your thumpy heart, spilling out, not blood, but light, neverending beams of it.

"I don't mean to make you uncomfort-able. But, before I met Owen's dad," she says, motioning her head toward the back-yard, "I dated my share of assholes and I know talking to another woman . . . helps. Men are *extremely* emotional, but they won't admit it to themselves! They hold it in . . . then kill their entire families before

157

killing themselves. It's out of control. Why won't they be honest with themselves instead of being such assholes? Men being honest with themselves and *truly* listening to women . . . it has the potential to change the world," she says.

"They only act like assholes so much because they can get away with it," you say.

"Well, men are gonna men. Fact. But it's not a woman's fault when a man behaves badly and it's not her job to fix him. And if you catch one waving that asshole flag, trust yourself and run! Without feeling bad about it," Owen's mom says.

"From here on out I will. I'll run," you agree, nodding. Owen's mom nods too.

And when you start to cry, Owen's mom gets up from the table. You put your face in your hands and let go. You've been holding everything in and Owen's mom makes you feel like you don't have to. She starts rubbing the place where your neck ends, where your back begins, that place moms somehow know to rub when you're crying or feeling sick. Her hand is warm and gentle. You take a shivery breath in. And out. In and out. In. And. Out.

"Oh, honey," Owen's mom says.

"I'm okay," you say.

"You're more than okay. You are just fine,"

Owen's mom says with hilly country comfort.

"Thank you for being so nice to me," you say, looking at her as she steps away from you to sit back at the table. You're embarrassed and hungry. You eat some more soup.

"Oh, please. Look. You're allowed to have a weird day. A weird week. A weird life!" she says, her laugh floating out of her mouth and popping like a bubble.

The female spirit solidarity healing spell is broken as Owen and his brother come back into the kitchen bringing along the dog behind them and some more laughter — the pleasant laundry-and-shampoo scent of recently showered boys.

"Nice to meet you," Malcolm says to you before heading toward the door. Malcolm is hulking. A Paul Bunyan in this summer kitchen.

"Where are you going?" his mom asks.

"Rugby. Park," he says, grabbing an apple from the fruit basket on the counter.

"Love you," his mom says.

"Love you, too," Malcolm says back.

"Best chicken tortilla soup you've ever had in your life, right?" Owen asks you, sitting at the table.

"Yes," you say.

You finish and thank Owen's mom again

before you and Owen leave to go get ice cream. Owen's mom hugs you and you let her, although you're not a big hugger. This is different. And you never get to see Owen's dad up close, but you see him cutting the backyard grass in a blue ball cap. Owen's fairytale backyard is edged with orange, yellow, and purple trumpet-flower bushes that attract butterflies. Seeing Owen's dad up close is something you can look forward to. Coming over again, talking to his mom for some more free kitchen table therapy, maybe even more chicken tortilla soup. You don't talk to your mom about your relationships and you rarely talk to your girlfriends about them because you are quiet and don't like bothering people and you rarely even open your heart to those you feel most comfortable with. You wish you and your mom were closer. You wish your mom was more like Owen's mom. You don't even know Owen's mom's name, so you ask Owen before you get in your car. He tells you and you say it aloud so your mouth can remember it.

On the way to the ice cream shop where you work, Owen tells you he sent Malcolm and Malcolm's rugby buddies over to Nick's place. To tell Nick not to bother you anymore. To leave you alone. Owen says they're not going to like, hit him or anything, but just let him know it's not cool and to stop it. You feel rescued although you hadn't been brave enough to come out and ask for it. Malcolm texts Owen as you're sitting with your ice creams outside of the shop. Owen shows you his phone, holds it straight out at you, proudly.

Done. He wasn't acting so tough with five dudes on his porch. Tell her to let us know if he ever bothers her again.

You get tears in your eyes. You cry easily. Owen is your new favorite friend. *Friend.* You think about the word, how pure and sweet it is. How it means so much, even though you take it for granted. The mystery of it. A person who will fight for you, protect you, lend an ear without expecting anything in return. You know there are good guys out there because Owen is proof. You want to write a poem about him, one he can keep in his back pocket and pull out and read aloud the way he does sometimes. You can't find the words to say thank you, but know Owen can *feel* them. Can probably taste that sweet-pink gratefulness in your ice cream as he takes a bite. You picture Nick with a purple-black eye, his wince-face, his tender arm in a sling. You like thinking Owen is keeping that violence from you, protecting you that way too. You think of how easily Owen threw Nick's phone. You picture it sinking and sinking down into the river until it can't sink any further. You picture yourself sinking and sinking down into the rushing, dirty-coin-colored river until you can't sink any further. You picture yourself rocketing out of the water in a flash of white light, right out of this vacuum-valley. You reach over to take a quick bite of Owen's ice cream and, like a mirror, you both put your hands on your foreheads and ow-laugh at your matching ice cream headaches. You're eating too fast, but you can't help it. You have to. You have to eat it all before it melts.

BRIGHT

The summer I stopped brushing again, let the wind dread my hair; we camped in the desert. Peed on sage. I wanted to eat sage, grow a squat sage bush inside of me, watch the roots scream-sprout from my ears, my fingers, my feet. Same summer we were in the forest when there was a cougar loose in Discovery Park. Hunting, its paws pressing heavy. Cracking sticks. Clicking brambles. Smushing grass. We made our way out of the trees and stopped at King's Hardware for Skee-Ball and tallboys of Vitamin R. Can you hear it — slick thump-rolling and bar chatterhum lifting? Can you hear the back door chunking closed? *Listen again.* No. Those are the drunk white boys at the campsite listening to Eazy-E, N.W.A. They're rapping, pretending to ride Jet Skis over the gravel. I made my girlfriends laugh when I called them chodes, but who were we to judge? If you dropped a record needle into the rock dust, Band of Horses would start playing. We ate salmon with lemons, drank beer for breakfast. Played *Marry, Fuck, or Kill* under the high noon sun. David Duchovny as Fox Mulder? *Always yesyes.* That evening it rained and rained. Goose bumps of rain popping on tent-skin. Branch scratches of rain on tent-roof. Drunken rain slipping down half-empty wine bottles, wild rain *ssss-ing* out campfires. We packed up in the morning, slicked our fingers over metal poles and cold-dripping canvas. Talked to sweatshirted strangers about the double rainbow hooping us. Watched an ant line of young girls in hippie nightgowns walk down a hill. I got drunk on the plane — flew out of Seattle rain into Nashville rain with the high, bright smell of desert sage drying me out, burning and burning.

DARK AND SWEET AND DIRTY

DARK: She wore a red dress, black tights, and crazy gold ankle-strap heels on their first date. A perfect outfit for drinking almost-too-strong IPAs and playing *Big Buck Hunter* with Clint, the guy she worked with at the camping store. They'd both turned twenty-one that summer, both home from different colleges until the fall semesters started. Their bearded, soft-bellied fathers worked together, too — associate pastors at the Baptist church on the corner. Their lives Venn diagramed, and there they were in the shaded area as friends–question mark who tried not to touch each other too much.

She pulled her last big chug of beer from the bottle. Clint held up his fingers, ordering two more. She looked at him, at the video game screen, him, the video game screen. The bar door bell was tinkling as people walked in, as people walked out.

166

Belle & Sebastian started playing, and she didn't feel right shooting things when Belle & Sebastian was playing. Too calm, too soothing. It didn't match up, so she put the gun back. She felt guilty about lusting over Clint. It was lazy, like cold French fries. It was because he was standing there in no socks with his skinny little ankles and skateboard sneakers and she just wanted a boyfriend.

He had the gun now and he was cocking and shooting and cocking and shooting at the screen. "I've never had coffee," she blurted out and stepped over to him. He turned and lifted his eyebrow.

"You've *never* had coffee?" he asked when his turn was over.

"That's not so weird, right? Lots of people haven't had coffee, I guess. It's one of those things that everyone *assumes* everyone has and loves all the time when really, lots of people haven't had it," she said.

"Wow. You've thought about this a lot. Like, you're defensive about it," he said. And it was so honest, it brought tears to her eyes, but she blinked them away and drank some more of her beer. She stood straighter because she wanted to look prettier. She wanted to look so pretty that he'd get stupid about it. She wanted to light herself up like

167

pretty incense and let her pretty smoke float around and up and hover over them.

"I've just never had coffee," she said softly. He picked up his beer.

"I hurt your feelings?" he asked, bent his head down and talked to her like she was a small, shaking puppy he'd brought home from the shelter. She kept expecting him to pet her. She *wanted* him to pet her.

"Kind of, but I know you didn't mean to."

"You're right. I'm sorry I called you defensive," he said. He kissed her cheek and she wasn't expecting it; his scruff, the sharp-swish of his face was against hers. The wet night was steaming up from the summer ground, she could see it from the window. She could feel it getting dark. Darker.

AND

SWEET: His parents weren't home and Clint said he'd make her coffee, but it might not be that good. And wouldn't she rather have it from a real coffee shop instead of a coffeemaker in his kitchen?

"No. I'd rather have it here," she said, slipping off her shoes and wandering around the kitchen and living room. His mom was the type to have those colorful drippy candles, scented volcanoes bleeding down thick glass bottles. She felt a headache coming on from sniffing them, so she stopped. And there were pictures of Clint all over the place because he was an only child. Two on the mantel taken right before and after his baptism. The long sleeves of his white gown stuck to his arms like petals.

"Here, Pioneer," Clint said, handing her a hot mug. She held it to her nose and smelled cinnamon. "I put all kinds of stuff in it. My mom makes hers sweet. My dad drinks his black. I figured since you're a girl . . ." He half shrugged and touched the point of her elbow. She said thank you. He finally told her she looked pretty. That her dress reminded him of the flowers in Texas. *"Clematis texensis,"* he said and she loved how his mouth moved when he said it. So much, even the tender skin underneath her eyelids twinkled. She tapped his black-jeaned hip with her free hand.

"I believe in this. I'm not some pissed-off preacher's kid. Are you?" she asked, nodding to the pictures and the ornate cross on the wall, pressing her palms tight around the mug so it could burn a little.

"I believe in it most of the time," he said, before drinking his coffee.

AND

169

DIRTY: She took a drink of hers and didn't hate it. It tasted like something dark and sweet and dirty. She told him that. Opened up and told him she wished she had an infinity of immortal fireflies in mason jars and an Australian accent although she was scared to go to Australia because she heard about the spiders. She liked how he looked at her like she was fucking crazy. It made her feel dark and sweet and dirty. And she didn't ask permission before walking down the glossy hallway in her black-tights-feet to his bedroom so she could check out his books. To see who he really was. She'd already made up her mind to go wild with him. The preachers' kids sinning up a storm, together; two beery baptized believers. A night for new things! He was the one, it was okay. This was it. And he wasn't Jesus or the devil or some monster. She had a vision of two empty white-as-snow hearts, refilling with red-black blood. She lay back on his pillow — soft as the lamb of God — and let go. Clean.

Felix Phoenix is a baseball player, a good one. I collect his dirty uniform after the games. Not only his — all the players' uniforms — but Felix Phoenix is my favorite. I am *missing* something by not being more involved in his life. That's why I go through his locker when the stadium lights are turned off and only the janitors and the cleaning ladies are here. The only thing I can tell from his uniform is how dirty he got during the game — whether he slid full on his belly or his butt. Sometimes, both — or his sides. I know he didn't have a good game if his uniform isn't dirty, if the home whites stay white, or even whitish. There are some players whose uniforms get super-dirty every time they play, no matter what. I smell Felix's uniform before I load it up for the cleaners. I even like his stink — hot wild onions in burnt brown-sugar dirt. I hold it to my nose and breathe in deep and I make sure no one sees me doing this because I know how creepy it is. I know! I don't need anyone to tell me. I don't need anyone to know. I also know I shouldn't go through his things, but I'm not hurting anyone and isn't that how we rationalize and measure whether or not what we're doing is truly wrong?

Q: AM I HURTING SOMEONE BY DOING WHAT I'M DOING?

  A: NO

Q: SO IS IT OKAY FOR ME TO GO ON AND KEEP DOING THE THING AS LONG AS THE OTHER PERSON DOESN'T FIND OUT AND AS LONG AS THE OTHER PERSON DOESN'T GET HURT?

  A: OF COURSE IT IS. IT'S FINE! YOU'RE FINE! AND EVEN IF IT IS CRAZY, IT'S ONLY SLIGHTLY CRAZY, SO YOU'RE STILL FINE!

I have a pen stuck in my hair and I slip it out and write YOU'RE STILL FINE on the back of my hand. Someone had dropped a crumpled piece of paper in front of Felix's locker and I bend down and grab it, determined to save it for later. I'll go home, make a too-hot bath and pour a glass of wine. Take my time getting in and once I am in, I'll look at the paper. Maybe it's a love note to me. Yeah right. But! He always says hi to me when he sees me. He always smiles too. I love his smile. It's Cheshire-cat-electric and looks like he's about to get into trouble. Or use it to get *out* of trouble. I see that smile when I close my eyes at night and think about him. Thinking about Felix is my favorite thing to do. Felix isn't married and neither am I and I'd marry Felix in a heartbeat, but he does have a girlfriend. I have already steeled my heart for the day he proposes because I worry he'll do it at the stadium and I'll have to work that night and see her name up on the scoreboard, hear her gasp when Felix and his out-of-this-world baseball thighs get down on one knee. I spend too much time thinking about whether or not Felix thinks I'm pretty. I look nothing like his girlfriend, so maybe he doesn't; maybe he's one of those guys who only thinks girls who look like his girlfriend are pretty. His girlfriend has straight hair and mine is curly. So curly I can put pens in it and forget they're even there until I wonder to myself *where did I put that dang pen* and start feeling around my head for it.

I keep double-checking my pocket to make sure the little piece of paper is in there and it is. It's probably nothing, but I want it, so I keep it. I've taken small things before. Once I took a tube of his Chapstick. Another time, a bottle cap. Things he would think he'd accidentally thrown away or would have eventually thrown away on purpose. I have the tube of Chapstick and I put it on every night before bed. And he's fine. He must've gotten a new one because his lips have never looked chapped, not even once. Something else Felix gave me that I keep is the one time he told me get home safe and I wasn't sure if he meant it as a baseball pun, but I think about it every time I leave work. I'm extra-careful because Felix told me get home safe once. And I think about it whenever I'm watching him play baseball and he's up at bat or stealing second or running from third to home on a wild pitch or an outfielder's error. *Get home safe, Felix Phoenix!*

I cry every time he gets a home run; he's hit forty-seven home runs so far this season. I've cried forty-seven times. The season is almost over. I keep checking my pocket for the piece of paper and wow I'm hoping it's something good because my back and arms are so sore from cleaning, and I can feel that hot-hot bathwater already. He didn't get a home run tonight so I won't get off. During the regular season I only get off on the days he hits home runs. On the days he hits a home run during playoffs, I do it twice. No getting off tonight, just the piece of paper with my wine and my bath and one cigarette too. On the regular season nights Felix doesn't hit a home run, I allow myself to have one pink Nat Sherman cigarette. I like to smoke that cigarette in the bathtub with my wine and I'm usually listening to some beautiful woman who has already gone to the great beyond gut-sing about how much she loved someone or how lonely she is. Like Bessie Smith or Big Mama Thornton or Koko Taylor or Billie Holiday. I've already decided on Billie Holiday for tonight, for the piece of paper. I'll light my candles. I love the tiny jump of a tealight! Obsessing over Felix Phoenix is my engine, my fireplace. And baseball is leaving us in October. It'll be getting cold soon and I'll curl up in front of that obsession fireplace and feel it warm on my face, the glow.

There was nothing else new in Felix's locker. He'd gone home already. A little girl had given him a fluffy brown teddy bear a year ago and some months later, that little girl died of cancer. Felix kept the brown teddy bear in his locker, and every night I'd take it out and smell its head and put it back exactly how I'd found it. The bear smelled like the expensive wood of the locker. I hang Felix's clean white uniform on the front of his locker with the back of it facing out. PHOENIX in shimmery gold. And I can't wait to get home, but I remember *get home safe,* so I drive the speed limit and don't go through any yellows. I stop completely at the stop signs in my neighborhood.

When I get naked at home, I eyeball that crumpled piece of paper on the bathroom counter and light the candles, turn off the lights. I go to the kitchen to get the bottle of red, the glass, my pack of cigarettes, and a lighter. I take my time getting in the water because it's so hot. I have the paper in one hand and use the other hand to pour myself a glass of wine. I take a big gulp because I want to *feel* it before I read the piece of paper. I take another big gulp and put the glass down. Billie Holiday is singing and singing and singing, her dusty paper-flower voice echoing off the tiled walls. I haven't eaten dinner and the bathwater is so hot I feel the wine almost immediately and say thank you, Dionysus aloud. I try to sing it along with Billie, but it doesn't fit. One of my cats comes in the bathroom to join me, the top of her tail happily hooked. I light my cigarette and wait for my eyes to fully adjust. I take a drag and inhale, finish my glass of wine, careful not to wet the paper.

"Okay, Felix," I say before I uncrumple it. I read it. I read it again. There's a goosebump party on my arms and my guts feel gnawed. I read it again and again and again before I take my lighter to it and watch most of it burn before dropping it in the steaming water.

[Rewind. Before I let the paper catch fire. Camera zooms in so the audience can read the black ink, the printing, the words.]

Felix it's your baby and you know it and you don't have to make this so difficult. A son has the right to know who his father is. Get your fucking shit together before I have this child. Tell your girlfriend or I will! GROW UP!

[The paper burns.]

I decide to smoke two cigarettes tonight because the piece of paper warrants two cigarettes and I'll allow myself to get off too, although it's technically cheating and not my usual home run celebration. I'll think about Felix and this faceless, nameless woman he got pregnant. It's official. Felix is a certified womanizer, so it's okay for me to think about Felix getting me pregnant too. I'd let him do whatever he wanted, I'd do whatever he wanted. I'd keep the baby or I'd have an abortion or shut up and go away and raise them alone, let him come visit them in secret, secretly bring them to his baseball games and whisper that's your daddy into their ear and point whenever Felix stepped up to the plate. Put them in a tiny Phoenix jersey. I would. I'd do whatever he wanted. Anything. Everything. And I knew burning the paper could hurt Felix, so I'd crossed the line. He would wonder what happened to it or who found it. It would worry him. But it was so careless of him to accidentally leave something like that lying around. That recklessness blew my hair back, made me love him more. He must be a mess. Maybe I can give him a signal. Maybe I can tell him I found a piece of paper on the floor outside his locker and I tossed it. Maybe I'll even give him a little wink so he can wonder what it means. What will he do then? I'll have to put on some of his Chapstick before I go online tonight to try and find out who this woman is. Who writes things on paper anymore? Whatever.

I'll reassure him I didn't even look at it. No, I would never look at it. I would never go through his things. That would be weird and I'm not like that. Nope, not me. Ew. And Felix will soften his face and ask me why I'm crying, but I won't know what to say.

Teenage Dream Time Machine

Today 8:35 p.m.

Ok, so where's Shelly?

In Cancun with her boyfriend.

Wow, really?

Oh girl, she bought the tiniest bikini the day their divorce was final.

This is the young guy she works with?

Yep. He's practically a fetus.

He's not!

He's 25.

Ok wow, he IS a fetus. I had no idea.

Both Keri and Hannah have a crush on him. Probably Claire too. I get it. He's really cute.

I always thought Shelly and Alex were happy together, but I know that's what everyone always thinks.

Do you think Mike and I are happy together?

Sure! You two seem like it.

We are! We are. I was just wondering if we seemed like it. Sometimes you can't tell.

Do Dave and I seem happy together?

Are you kidding me? Dave thinks you're the only woman God created. I know you two are happy together. You, what, met in elementary school or something?

Middle school.

Same thing. It's pretty much law that you two have to stay together. If y'all break up, I'll kill myself.

Stop it.

You think I'm kidding.

I was worried you and Shelly were mad at me after the girls snuck out.

Mad at you? For what?

For not keeping a close enough eye on them . . . like it was our fault.

Oh, please. Those girls had that planned out. How would you know?

I just still feel guilty, that's all.

Well, you've got to let that go. It could've been any one of us and I'm just thankful nothing really happened. They weren't even out there that long. None of them got pregnant, none of them got hit by a train . . .

Dave said they were terrified when he showed up. He'd gotten up to get a glass of water and decided to peek in on the girls, to make sure the window was closed since he'd turned the AC on. And the girls were gone. He didn't even wake me up, he just put on a shirt and went out and found them. He couldn't say how he knew where they were, he just . . . knew. I woke up to an empty house and went out on the front porch in a panic, saw Dave and the girls coming up the sidewalk. The girls were

182

crying. Dave had his stern face on, but I could see the twinkle in the corners of his eyes. I could tell.

I did shit like that all the time when I was their age. Worse, even. I'm not worried about those girls a bit.

Not even a little?

Not even a little.

I told Claire she's grounded for at least a week. Maybe longer. I haven't decided yet.

Keri's grounded for a week too. And Hannah's at her dad's anyway since Shelly's in Cancun.

Would you go back . . . if you could . . . be that age again?

What, if I had some kind of teenage dream time machine?

Exactly.

I was fourteen in 1992. So we're talking what . . . Boyz II Men, Kris Kross, "To Be with You" by Mr. Big? I listen to them and that's enough time machine for me. Oh, and "November Rain" by GnR. Also, Trey Brown shoving his tongue down my throat at the skating rink.

I was fourteen in 1990. Just bones and legs and hair. I must've gone through a can of White Rain a week. I loved Roxette. Oh and "Black Velvet" by Alannah Myles! Dave was forever shoving his tongue down my throat at our locker.

You two! And wow, I love that song so much. Also, Paula Abdul, Janet Jackson, Whitney Houston . . . those are my jams. And I wore two pairs of socks with my Keds! I can't even remember why. LOL. Oh and scrunchies! Everything was scrunchies. And jellies. I loved my jellies. I was a cheerleader! Were you a cheerleader?!

I loved my jellies too! I remember how they used to smell! And no. I wasn't a cheerleader. I wasn't nearly that cool! LOL.

I was only cool for like, a minute. :) Btw, I lost my virginity to "I'll Make Love to You" by Boyz II Men. I mean, wow.

Dave and I were listening to DEF LEPPARD.

POUR SOME SUGAR ON ME?!

Of course! LOL.

I love it. Did you ever dye your hair?

Bright pink once and my mom almost killed me. I used to spray Sun In in my hair when I laid out, but it didn't do much. It smelled good though. I wanted to be Drew Barrymore. I wanted to be Courtney Love for a minute too.

Same. This is so funny . . . all the women our age . . . we were practically living the same life! We're all connected . . . like magic.

Exactly like magic. We don't even need a teenage dream time machine! LOL.

LOL. But wow NO! I wouldn't go back to being a teenager though. All that insecurity and acne? Never.

NEVER. Praise the Lord! We've got such beautiful, good girls.

They are wildly beautiful. And even when they're a little bad, they're still pretty good.

And they have each other.

185

And so do we.

You couldn't pay me to go back.

Not even if we had a hot-pink teenage dream time machine!

With glitter all over it!

And it'd smell like Love's Baby Soft.

And that Debbie Gibson perfume I had.

Electric Youth!

And Exclamation!

Wow, I'd forgotten about that one.

Ooh and Jean Nate!

Ok, I really forgot about that one!

I used to sneak in my mom's room and put it on.

I used to sneak and read my parents' copy of Joy of Sex.

LOL! I did the same thing!

Let's put a copy of that in the teenage dream time machine. The one from the 70s with the armpit hair!

Totally hot. Also, I had a crush on Keanu Reeves!

So did I! And both Jason Priestley AND Luke Perry!

Absolutely the 90210 boys! And Mark-Paul Gosselaar! And girl, Eddie Vedder. I would've done ANYTHING for Eddie. And I mean ANYTHING.

Exact same. Oh and I also had the BIGGEST crush on Dwayne Wayne from A Different World!

ME TOO.

Wow, ok. While we're talking about it, I wouldn't mind having my teenage body back.

Girl, tell me about it.

Girl. Would you marry Dave all over again?

I would . . . isn't that disgusting?

187

It's not disgusting! It's amazing and super-romantic. It's the dream!

Would you marry Mike again?

I don't think so . . . but it's ok! Really, it's ok. We're happy and it's ok. And we have Keri.

And she's a gem.

She is. And so is Claire. And Hannah too!

We really do have the best girls.

The best girls. They're into the skateboarders now, by the way.

Ah, that's right. That Milo boy is a skate-boarder.

I'd maybe go back for the skateboarders.

Only for the skateboarders?

Yes! The skateboarders were always my fave. They're cocky and cute and they throw the best parties, they have the best hair, the best shoes . . .

I missed out. I never dated a skateboarder!

Well, you have Dave and he's a motorcycle guy.

Totally a motorcycle guy. What's Mike? Was he a skateboarder?

Mathlete!

Aw, yay! So was I! Nerds unite!

LOL. Keep an eye out for the skateboarders rolling through your neighborhood because our girls are watching them. Like hawks.

Good thing we can hear them coming, right?

Right! LOL!

I'm just really sorry the girls snuck out of our house. I still feel bad about that.

Will you stop?

Ok, ok. I'm sorry!

STOP APOLOGIZING.

I WILL. I promise I will.

Good! You're a good mom. And I know those

boys were scared to death once they saw Dave. LOL.

Fersure. And no, you . . . YOU'RE a good mom!

We've got to stick together!

Absolutely! Can you BELIEVE we're the moms now? Oh no . . . are we old?

No! FACT: we're young and beautiful and will remain forever so.

Yes! Ok. I'll remember that.

Next time we go out let's make up a drink called TEENAGE DREAM TIME MACHINE!

It needs to taste like champagne and peaches!

And cherries and Lip Smackers!

It should probably be a slushie, too.

And come with an expensive night serum. LOL.

Perfect. And boys aren't allowed to drink it. LOL.

No boys allowed!

Not even the skateboarders?

Not even the skateboarders!

Girls only.

That's right. Girls only.

Forever.

Wow I love you.

I love you too. We're heading out of town next week but talk when we get back? Maybe we should plan a giant slumber party with the girls and do face masks and nails and watch Molly Ringwald movies. The girls will be mortified . . . it'll be perfect! Oh and when Shelly is finished getting her groove back with the fetus, catch her up on our TEENAGE DREAM TIME MACHINE drink . . . ask her what else we need to add to it!

THIS SOUNDS LIKE SO MUCH FUN. Yes! I will! Be safe. Talk soon!

Rope Burns

Bridge Blackfeather takes me to the rodeo, cowboy church. Passes the buttery popcorn salt crystals from his tongue to mine while our boots slide heavy on the peanut-shelled hush-dusty floor. I am wearin' a dark denim jacket with a long black dress, my thick, titian tantrum of hair stormin' down my back. Bridge tells me it reminds him of the wild horses, pets me real slow and careful-like so I won't bite. But I do. I snap and nip at his fingers to make him laugh. Clink his gold initial ring between my teeth. I grew my armpit hair out for him and he gets inside my jacket to pet that too. Points to the cowboy, the buckin' bronco and says that's me and you and I don't ask which is which because I don't want him to tell me. Knowin' is a knife. We met way back. Summer, teenagers. Stood in my sultry kitchen when my parents weren't home, both of us as frenzied as them river-green junebugs

192

slammin' into the window screen. My bikini bottom like a rain-wet petal stickin' to the counter as we kissed hard. Two dirty dishrag mouths, wringin' out. Hummin' yellow summer afternoons: numberless, sweaty, clandestine. We ate slippery vegetable sandwiches afterward. Left the sunporch smellin' like the steam of sex and oily artichokes. We tied our high school heart ropes together. Real tight. I have the rope burns to show for it. Before bed, Bridge takes off his shirt to reveal his tattooed proof, my first name, an eighteen-year-old wink of night-black ink on amber milk-cream. Tempestuous lasso loopin' cursive. I've told everyone, I'll tell you. I married Bridge because he's thunder. That man right there is a pack of hungry wolves howlin' at the moon. I'm still enchanted by the white-flicker flame shiverin' and achin' against the cave wall of his hands when he lights his cigarettes. The bright violet glow of his superheated supplication as he bows his head, finds harbor. He kitten-licks me like he's thirsty, dyin', like I hold cool livin' water in my collarbone cups.

GET FAYE & BIRDIE

To: Birdie Taylor-Boone
From: Faye Taylor
Date: September 13, 2020, 9:02 a.m.
Subject: MENARETRASH

Bird,

Hi baby! When you were little and would ask, I liked to tell you that your first word was MENARETRASH and you'd roll your eyes and say, *Mama that's three words not one,* because you're a cute little smart ass. You're a cute little smart ass because I raised you like that. And not to brag, but I did a really good job. Agreed? I'm saying this because back when I swore off men, I kept hearing your baby voice saying MENARE-TRASH.

Also, it's too quiet here without you.

I know how much you hate talking on the phone, so I email you when I want to talk. I still want to hear your voice at least every other week. FaceTiming your mom a couple times a month isn't too much to ask! I'll kick the guilt into overdrive if necessary. You know I will! Also, forgive me when my emails are overly sentimental, which will be every time. It's what mamas do. I miss you! Can't believe you're in college already. Tell me all about forensics please! I want to know everything!

The art show is next week and I'm almost ready. By almost ready I mean I still have a ton of earrings and necklaces to make, but your Auntie Kim helps and she's such good company. She sends her love, always. She can't believe you're so grown up either! I don't know how I would've made it without her throwing her arms around me like a sister back when I was pregnant with you. Women can be so good about taking care of each other, it makes me want to cry every day!

So, tell me how you and Alayna are! How long has it been since I've told you how much I love that you don't have to deal with men? You're my perfect daughter. I can't wait until you two come home next month for fall break and we can make lasagna and watch *Mamma*

Mia! The girl in the movie could've been you looking for her daddy like that! You know I'm kidding, but it's funny because it's true!

I love you so much. More than you'll ever know. I've loved you hard and crazy since the moment I peed on that stick. I peed on four sticks to make extra sure! Write soon please. Don't break your mama's heart.

Lovelove you,
Your Mama

To: Faye Taylor
From: Birdie Taylor-Boone
Date: September 13, 2020, 11:45 p.m.
Subject: Re: MENARETRASH

Hi Mama,
I don't take real forensic courses until sophomore year. This year is mostly chem and bio. Junior year I get to take forensic chem and lab. The actual fun stuff. I'll keep you posted, but you have to admit how your eyes glaze over once I start talking science. Remember when you literally fell asleep on me that time I was talking about fluorescent powders??? I just started laughing so hard I had to stop typing for a second. My roommate

is going to think I'm nuts more than she already does! LOL.

Of course I will FaceTime you soon. I'm okay with talking on the phone sometimes and I love texting . . . so text me too! But, I do think it's sweet we can write to each other like this. I miss you!

You know how chill and happy Alayna and I are together. We want to get married after we graduate. I'm thinking of taking her name. How's Birdie Valentino sound? But yeah, we have plenty of time to talk about that. We're not rushing anything. And I'm glad you're not worried about us being too serious too fast anymore. Our relationship is the same level of comfy and sweet it's always been. I'm lucky! Please don't hate on high school sweethearts just because of Jack Boone.

Wow, Jack Boone. Feels kind of crazy writing his name in an email . . . but whenever I think about him now, I let myself . . . without trying to stop it. And something else. Over the summer . . . Uncle Coot told me that the man who killed Jack died in prison. I didn't say anything to you about it back then because I knew you might not feel like discussing it. Is it okay to talk about?

Do you want to talk about it?

And as much as I know you'd LOVE to take credit for my lesbianism, I'm sorry (not sorry) to say again that it wasn't the MENARETRASH thing that did it. I know you're half-kidding when you say it, but I'm a lesbian because I am. It's not a reaction to your life or to men. Shocker: it has nothing to do with men at all and everything to do with women and me. Who I am.

I hope the art show is perfect. Tell Auntie Kim I said hi! Send me pictures and let me know how it goes! I'm wearing a pair of your earrings tonight — the big, gold leaves to celebrate autumn coming soon.

You do have me beat, but just so you know, I have plenty of sentimental moments too. I heard "Super Trouper" the other day and cried in the coffee shop, because I was so homesick for Kentucky and missed you. You're such a good mama and I'm so glad you're mine.

Lovelove you,
Bird

PS: Alayna loves your lasagna!

To: Birdie Taylor-Boone
From: Faye Taylor
Date: September 14, 2020, 8:03 a.m.
Subject: Re: MENARETRASH

Birdie Louise Valentino is so beautiful and I'm already thinking of what color dress I will wear! (Birdie Louise Taylor-Valentino is pretty too, since you knew I'd throw that in!) And I do like to think that I at least had *some* sort of influence on your life with the new word I invented: MENARETRASH, but yes, of course, I know you are who you are. I've always known! That's why you never had to come out to me. You've always been and always will be my free little Birdie.

I bring it up sometimes, but I do regret giving you your daddy's last name. I should've named you Birdie Louise Taylor. I only went with Taylor-Boone to honor him since Jack died when I was pregnant and your grandmother wanted me to. She'd been so nice to me and had just lost Jack, and I felt bad for her. She's a sweet woman. She told me she sent you a care package! Was it full of candy and books? I bet she sent you more candy than I did. She's never been shy about spoiling you rotten. Mama's com-

199

ing down for the art show . . . she's sending you something soon too. :)

And yeah . . . well, I'm glad your Uncle Coot told you that somebody killed Johnny Step in prison. Finding out about that brought up a lot of bad memories, but . . . I don't mind talking about it now. Men who live like that die like that. That's in the Bible.

Bird, I'll never regret your daddy because part of him gave me YOU, my light! Once I laid eyes on you, I knew you were Jack's because you were a Boone baby through and through. Undeniable. If you want to talk about Jack Boone we can talk about Jack Boone. I've always been honest with you about everything. I was ashamed to tell you those things, but I told you anyway. Even when it hurt. And I let him hurt me . . . a lot . . . back then when I was living in the dark. No more! No more. ♡

But girl, if I had a time machine I'd tell myself this: Faye, you don't need him! Just light his shit on fire before you leave!

Lovelove,
Mama

Mama, you're my light, too! Aaand my corny cheeseball. ;)

I don't mind talking/hearing about Jack Boone either. And I love that you've always let me call him Jack Boone because it felt weird for me to call him Dad or Daddy or Rowdy, when I never even met him. And from what I've heard from everyone except Grandma, he didn't sound like somebody worth meeting. Uncle Coot told me once that Jack was really good at poker. And so am I. Of all the things to get passed down, that's not such a bad one. Grandma always talks about how I have Jack's eyes. You've told me that my whole life. Every time we go back to town, a different person tells me that.

Yep, Grandma Boone's care package was full of candy, books, and cookies. She sent me that North Carolina bird encyclopedia I'd been talking about with a little note that said *birds for Birdie* and some wool socks too. Pretty much all of my socks are from Grandma Boone!

Lovelove,
Bird

To: Birdie Taylor-Boone
From: Faye Taylor
Date: September 14, 2020, 1:52 p.m.
Subject: Re: MENARETRASH

Let me tell you . . . when I packed up and left that town I kept thinking of "This Woman's Work" by Kate Bush. Listen to it. I kept thinking about how what I was doing was "This Woman's Work." All of it. I'm sorry you never got to meet your daddy; I'm sorry he never even knew I was pregnant. My Woman's Work was when I got myself all ready to tell him when he came home, but he never got there because the cops picked him up. And when he got out of jail that time, he was so mad at me and hating the world, I didn't feel safe around him anymore. I didn't want him near me when he was like that. I told you how he came home and broke every plate in the kitchen and about tore the door off the hinges. Screamed at me to quit crying, but I couldn't stop. One of those guys in jail told him all kinds of nasty things about me, but I wasn't going to let Jack hurt me for it. I don't know why it took me so long to draw that line, but I'm glad I drew it. Classic Jack to go missing for a week then pop up again and get into it with those monsters. Classic Jack, ending up on the wrong side of a gun like some dark-holler country song.

I've told you before that I don't think Jack could've been a good father, no matter how hard he tried. He didn't have it in him. Your Grandma Boone said as much. I'll never forget her on that porch looking me right in the eyes and saying Jack tries, but he just can't. I went ahead and asked her just can't what and she said Faye Louise, he just can't.

Listen to a mother when she tells you about her child. Mamas know.

Jack was good at poker, yes. Too good. Gambling always got him into trouble. And Johnny . . . wow, Johnny was a terrible man, way worse than Jack, but I'm not taking up for Jack Boone. I learned my lesson there. Just because he's dead doesn't mean I'll sit here and say he was a good man, because he wasn't. I used to think he *could've* been a good man if he'd wanted to. I fell in love with that delusion.

Few times a year he'd get all cleaned up on Sunday morning for church, sober and smiling. But Lord have mercy . . . hell would break loose again. Saturday night always rolled around quick no matter what. And that was the real him: Saturday Night Jack. I was so obsessed with him in high school thinking he was this dreamy bad boy when really, he was just . . . bad. He was my first love, but the Jack I loved didn't even exist. My biggest blessing besides you was growing up and out of those lies I kept telling myself.

If I had to think of something nice to say about him I'd say he made good spaghetti sauce and his laugh was so goofy it made everyone in the room laugh along with him. And you've seen plenty of pictures, so you know how cute he was. Girl . . . those eyes got me. Not only do I see him in your out-of-this-world gorgeous eyes . . . but also in the little sighs you make while you're sleeping. You got what was good about him and that was the best thing he ever did . . . passing those things on to you.

I tried like hell to keep Jack from the end I knew in my bones was coming. I think about those months before I got pregnant with you . . . when I thought he would change . . . keep a decent job. Stupidly believing he'd stopped gambling and running with those monsters. I shouldn't have been surprised, but I was and I was wrong. Dead wrong! I've never been more wrong about anything in my life. It was arrogant of me to think that somehow I could make him a better man than he was. Why me? Ain't nobody that special.

Grandmommy and Granddaddy helped all they could, but if your Uncle Coot hadn't given me that money to leave town and move on, who knows what would've happened? Uncle Coot loves you so much. He finished your bookcase! I'll send a picture soon. I told him he was going to have to make another one with how much you read. It looks good in your bedroom, right by the window. Sometimes I go in and look at it because it's so pretty and I miss you so much. Your room still smells like you. Apples!

To: Faye Taylor
From: Birdie Taylor-Boone
Date: September 14, 2020, 7:12 p.m.
Subject: Re: MENARETRASH

Mama, you ARE special. That doesn't change just because guys are assholes. ;)
More soon, I promise. I'm so hungry! Gonna go find fries!

To: Birdie Taylor-Boone
From: Faye Taylor
Date: September 14, 2020, 10:05 p.m.
Subject: Re: MENARETRASH

Ha! Yeah . . . I never made those same mistakes with any men (assholes) after Jack. Sacrificing my heart, soul, and body. That's why I never got married, why I never brought any other men into your life besides Uncle Coot. He's one of the good ones.
I wasted too much time . . . women waste so much time on men who aren't worth it! It's infuriating and I still get angry with myself. :\ If somebody would've told me when I was younger that I would be single and happy in my forties, I would've about laughed myself to death. And ta-da! Here I am! Whew.
I know you and Alayna aren't me and Jack. Far from it. Please do give her my love. ♡
Study hard! Be safe! Crank ABBA! Just because you're a vegetarian doesn't

mean you can eat fries for every meal! Eat some vegetables, please. For me?

Thank you so much for telling me I've been a good mama, because that's certainly what I set out to do. You're my only baby and I never wanted to mess this up. See? Sentimental! And yes, I'm crying.

To: Faye Taylor
From: Birdie Taylor-Boone
Date: September 15, 2020, 12:04 a.m.
Subject: Re: MENARETRASH

I know how much you regret the dumb stuff you did when you were younger. All I see when I look at you is a strong, true, woman, artist, and mother who turned her life around. I'm strong and honest because you taught me how to be. Do you know how much I admire you for telling me everything yourself and not trying to hide it? Not many people would do that. Told you that you were special. I meant it. ♡ Aw, YAY. I love Uncle Coot foreverrrr. I'll text him about the bookcase soon! Stoked to see it in person.

The fries were delicious by the way. Fries before guys, fries before girls, fries before emails! :P

And I mean, don't get me wrong. I live in this world. Duh. Granddaddy and Uncle Coot aside, obviously I know MENARETRASH. :p

To: Birdie Taylor-Boone
From: Faye Taylor
Date: September 15, 2020, 8:33 a.m.
Subject: Re: MENARETRASH

LOL! That's my girl! :D Have I told you that you're my favorite daughter?

Counting down the days until I see your pretty face!

THE DARL INN

My mom was having sex with her new boyfriend and I was so used to it, it didn't even gross me out anymore. She said she'd let us share a beer if Bri and I promised not to come back to the room for at least two hours. We went and sat in the chairs outside by the pool, passed the bottle back and forth, made the mouth of it taste like our pineapple lipgloss. Once we'd finished drinking, I set the bottle down and it rolled on its side; the hollow-emptiness rattled as it slipped into the wet grass.

No one was at the pool even though it was Friday night. I figured there would at least be some dumb guys to flirt with. Maybe even some smart ones. The guys we went to high school with were pretty smart, but they acted dumb. Maybe that's how everyone was. I hypnotized myself thinking about it — watched the blue-green water lick up the pool steps, shiver in the motel light.

209

Bri's mom and my mom had been best friends since high school and Bri's mom traveled a lot for work. We'd been best friends since we were in utero, like Jesus and John the Baptist. Bri's dad was rarely around, so she stayed with my mom and me most weekends. We only lived like an hour away, but this weekend my mom said she wanted to get out of town, see something different. "Don't take being alive for granted, girls," she said.

We drove to this little town in the country called Darling and got a cheap room at the Darling Inn. I thought it'd be better if they called it the Darl Inn and it was kind of driving me crazy. I wanted to say something to the receptionist lady about it, but she was grumpy and wearing all brown, so I passed.

"Whitney, listen to this," Bri said, reading aloud from an old *Cosmo* magazine we'd found in the room. I watched the orange sunset glowing in her rhinestone-rimmed sunglasses. *My* sunglasses. I'd gotten them last summer from a grocery store in Vegas when I was out there visiting my dad. "Top Ten Things Guys Hate," she said, lifting the sunglasses so I could see her roll her eyes.

"Let me guess . . . um, girls who read those lists. No, no. Wait, don't tell me!

Ummm, how about we don't care what they hate because we can do whatever we want?" I said. Bri snickered like a little cartoon chipmunk.

We played the game we always played where one of us would open the magazine to a random page and we'd both pick our most and least favorite outfits.

"This dress is so pretty I hate it," I said, tapping my finger on a thistle-colored dress with tiny embroidered hummingbirds swooping over one shoulder.

"Murder me if I ever wear something this ugly," Bri said, poking the glossy picture of some H-list actress in a dark yellow jumper and matching espadrilles.

"If this pool was fucking empty I'd skate in it," someone said and we turned to see some SoCal-looking guys walking through the fence gate — big T-shirts, long, baggy dark-colored shorts, bony hairy guy legs slipped into well-worn skateboarder shoes. All three of them were carrying skateboards. Two of the guys were wearing shadowy T-shirts with monsters on them and the other one was wearing a plain white one, bright as eggs.

"What's up?" one of the guys said to us. He had on the forest-green shirt with a gray outline of Bigfoot walking across it. He had beer-blond hair and looked like he'd just woken up.

I was wearing a tiny tie-dye bikini and sat up a little straighter, readjusted my straps.

"Who are you guys?" another one of the dudes said. His shirt had some kind of winged dinosaur bird on it with lots of teeth.

"Well, for one, we're girls. Not guys," Bri said, closing the magazine and slapping it across her stomach. She pointed at her boobs with her thumb.

"Obviously," he said.

"Obviously," she said, laughing at him.

"I'm Whitney. She's Bri," I said to the one in the white shirt who hadn't said anything yet. I liked him the most. He looked like the kind of guy who would help you load groceries into your car without being a creep about it. He pointed to himself and said Jay and he motioned to the monster shirt guys and said Jesse and Jimmy.

"You're kidding me. Ugh, *all* of your names start with J?" Bri said. She pushed her sunglasses on top of her head.

"Getting kind of dark for shades, you think?" Jimmy said. He dropped his skateboard on the concrete and sat on it. He rolled back and forth and I liked the sound — chunky, growly. It sounded like such a dude sound to make.

"That's why I took them off, asshole," Bri said. She was flirting, but it was probably lost on the guys. Bri's heart was as hard as a diamond, but it was just as sparkly, too. I loved her so much I barely noticed she was around.

"Where are you from?" Jay asked me.

"Not here," I said, laughing a little bit.

"Figured."

"What about y'all?"

"My dad owns this piece of shit motel," Jay said with that comforting Kentucky coal miner's lilt. He smirked, real cute. I liked looking at his face. Jimi Hendrix's version of "The Star-Spangled Banner" started playing in my head when I looked at him. He was so gloriously American, I had to keep myself from standing and putting my hand over my heart.

"Okay, good ol' boy. You need to tell your dad to change the name of this place to the Darl Inn instead of the Darling Inn. Get it? Darl Inn? It's annoying it's not called the Darl Inn. I can barely stay here. I'd want to leave if the vending machines weren't so awesome. That one has the spicy chips I like," I said, pointing across the pool. Bri and I had dyed the tips of our hair soft peony-pink with my mom's help. I tucked a pale slip of it behind my ear.

"The Darl Inn," Jay said and nodded.

"The Darl Inn," Bri repeated.

I looked at the motel sign buzzing up by the road. It was super-pretty. The D was big, old-timey cursive and a dreamy blue color. Maybe that was the color I'd dye my hair next.

"I like it. Your hair," Jesse said to us, pointing at his own head. It was the first thing that had come out of his mouth.

"Thanks," I said. Bri stood from the chair and walked to the pool — took the steps real slow like she was in a beauty pageant. She was cracking me up, so I laughed and laughed and shook my head.

"Hey, Jesse James, why do you bring your skateboard to a pool?" Bri asked.

Jesse shrugged. Jimmy started talking. "Why do you keep such a smart mouth all the time? Damn, girl," he said.

"How old are you losers?" Bri asked, ignoring him. She floated on her back and moved her arms, made snow angels in the water. The sun was hissing out behind the hills. The green-glowy pool lights came on with a soft click — a tender, intimate sound that made me ache for somewhere else. I wanted to drive to California in a gold Camaro with Bri. We'd stop and buy shotguns and gas station lipsticks, blast "American

214

Woman" and "Barracuda" as we drove through the desert.

"Same age as you, probably," Jay said, "sixteen."

I nodded. "She'll be seventeen next month. So will I."

Jay said they came down to the pool every Friday night, but usually it was moms with their kids and old guys smoking, trying to get drunk on cheap light beer.

"We're just passing through," I said.

"You seem like the type to pass through," he said back to me. I liked how he said it, like we were in a movie and I was mysterious.

Bri was still floating and I stood, knowing the boys were watching every part of me. I walked around, did my prettiest dive into the deep end of the pool. I sank and held my breath as long as I could.

YOU SHOULD LOVE
THE RIGHT THINGS

Not how it hurts when you press down on a yellowish-blue, purple-black bruise, but the feeling you get when you lift up. Let go.

And Down We Go!

Sierra is wearing Doug's oversized Led Zeppelin T-shirt. So black it is nothing. The color matches the smudged rims of her eyes. She considers washing her face before she leaves his apartment, but he's in the bathroom now and she wants to get out of there.

"Doug, I'm wearing your shirt. I spilled wine on mine last night," she says loudly after she taps, tells him she is leaving. She looks down, zips and buttons her jeans.

"Cool. I'll wash it for you," he says with a muffled toothpaste-mouth. He opens the door.

"I'll give you a call later?" she says, that question mark hanging over them both, like a puff of gray-white smoke.

"Yeah?" he says. The puff grows. The puff is now a dust tornado.

"Yeah, okay!" she says, adjusting her purse strap up on her shoulder before that tornado blows the whole effing apartment building down.

She is alone now. She smooths her hair and goes in her purse for her compact as the elevator rattles and drops a floor. She licks her finger and wipes some of the eyeliner from underneath her eyes. Reapplies her lipgloss and checks her phone for the time. When the elevator doors open, she has to grit her teeth. She hates Brooks Clark and there he is dressed in his annoyingly perfectly fitting suit with his annoyingly perfectly shined shoes and he doesn't even look up from his phone as he steps onto the elevator. He stands there scrolling and scrolling and she finally has to ask him if he's going all the way down.

"Oh. My bad. Thanks. Yeah, I'm heading down to the lobby," he says, not looking up at her. And duh, of course he is going to the lobby, why wouldn't he be going to the lobby?

The glowing yellow circle labeled *L* is already lit up, so she doesn't have to do anything. The doors shut and the elevator drops again. Sierra can't help herself from checking out Brooks's watch and the cuffs of his sleeves and she takes a quick breath to check if he smells good and he does. *Entitled asshole.*

She sees him laugh at something he reads on his phone and he reaches up to massage his temple before putting his phone in his pocket. He's probably hungover and woke up with some strange woman in his bed. *Dickhead.* The elevator lights flicker and shut off, the big metal box they are standing in shakes and comes to a stop. Sierra can hear the screech of an alarm somewhere in the distance. Her heart, her blood, is surely making the same sound, trapped tightly inside of her.

"Shit," Brooks says into the darkness. Sierra figures some emergency lights will be kicking on soon but right now, nothing. Just deep, static-black and aloneness with some dickhead guy who is a friend of her brother's.

"I'm sure they'll fix it soon," she says, more to herself than to him. She wants to keep calm. She uses the same breathing technique that comes in handy whenever she feels a panic attack rising at the dentist or in large crowds.

"Last time it was out like this, it took three hours. It was some *bullshit,*" he says. The way he says it makes her want to laugh, but she won't give him the pleasure. He sounds so annoyed, it's hilarious. He doesn't sound scared.

"It's Sierra. Tyler's sister, by the way. You didn't look up from your phone when you got on the elevator so . . . ," she says in her bitchiest voice.

"Wow. Forreal? Hey, how are you? *Where* are you?" He laughs. She feels his hand graze her arm and she grabs his wrist, hard.

"I'm right here," she says, pushing his wrist back to him. "Will they turn the lights on?"

"They'll turn them on," he says plainly. She hates him, but wishes she could see his face so she could read his expression. She takes a seat in the corner because sitting makes her less anxious. A voice booms through the elevator's intercom system. Neither of them is using their phone flashlights and it is oddly pleasing. She feels a bite of satisfaction. She isn't going to be the first one to pull her phone out.

"Is there anyone on the elevator?" the voice says.

"Yes. Brooks Clark from 6D and one other person. A woman. Um, Sierra Mitchell. From . . ."

"My boyfriend, Doug Wilder, lives in 7A," Sierra rolls her eyes, even though it is too dark for Brooks to see. She hears him sit down. Wonders if he will fuss about getting his precious pants dirty.

"The drummer from NightVision?" Brooks asks.

"Yes!" she says. She huffs and puffs like a wolf.

"Hello, Mr. Clark. Our apologies. And apologies to you as well, Ms. Mitchell. Doug's a good guy. Their new album is really good . . . yeah." The voice pauses awkwardly. "We'll . . . um . . . get y'all to where you need to be very shortly. Pardon the interruption," the voice says.

Sierra is teetering on the edge of a full-on tantrum and it's hot in the elevator. As stuffy and claustrophobic as she ever imagined the nightmare of a stuck elevator to be. She is scared to be there, she hates Brooks. She raises her voice when she asks the speaker guy how long he thinks it'll be until the elevator is working.

"Won't be too long, I promise. You guys sit tight, okay?" the speaker guy says as if they have a choice. He clicks off.

"Wait. What about the lights?" Sierra says to nothing.

"They should come on in a sec," Brooks says. And like he is God or something, the emergency lights flash on above them. They are unnaturally white and too-bright and there are only two of them casting shaky submarine-light across their faces. Brooks smiles at her. Sierra's stomach drops like a broken elevator.

Something did and didn't happen when they were in college. One night, Brooks had given her a ride home. He pulled up in front of her apartment and put his car in park.

"You can come upstairs if you want to. I mean, I'm drunk, but . . . ," she said, pretending to be more drunk than she was. She wanted to see what he'd say and if it didn't go her way she'd claim she had no idea what he was talking about.

"I can't. Actually, I have to go pick up my grandmother from the airport," Brooks said.

Sierra opened the door and said fine. He reached for her, put his hand on her leg until she moved.

"Wait," he said.

"Fuck off, Brooks," she said.

"You don't believe me? Come with me, then. Come with me to pick up my little old grandmother from the airport," he said. He put his hand back on her leg.

She snatched herself out of the car, stepped into the cold. Brooks rolled down his window.

"What's up?"

"Goodbye, Brooks," she replied, saying his name like it tasted gross in her mouth, something she couldn't wait to spit out.

One in the morning, he was back at her door. His clothes looked impossibly neat. He was bright-eyed and smiling. Sierra was half-drunk, rubbing her eyes. She asked him what he was doing there.

"I took my grandmother home and got her settled. Her flight was late. *Aaand* she's a talker," he said, leaning against the door frame.

"I was asleep," she said.

"I figured," he said, motioning to her T-shirt and underwear. She tugged her shirt down so it would cover her bottom as she walked backward to the bedroom to retrieve a pair of pajama pants. Brooks turned to lock the door behind him and looked around her living room, inspecting things in the Christmas-tree light.

On the elevator, Sierra doesn't want to seem interested in Brooks. That would be the worst. He is arrogant, a womanizer. She's heard too many stories from her brother, from her friends. He hasn't always been a gentleman. Fuck that. He's a douche. The emergency lights are too harsh on both their faces and she half wishes they'd go off again. The elevator is even hotter now. Her phone no longer has reception.

"Is your phone working?" she asks him.

"Nah," he says, shaking his head.

"This place is too nice to have a jacked-up elevator."

"Ain't that the truth."

If she doesn't say anything else, maybe he'll be quiet until they get the elevator fixed. The thought annoys her. Is it too much to ask for him to *not* be an asshole for once? Is it too much to ask for him to initiate conversation?

And Doug? Doug won't worry about her for at least a day. He never takes the elevator unless he has to. He is one of those freaks who takes the stairs unless he's carrying a ton of stuff. He'll never know the elevator is stuck and he isn't expecting Sierra to text or call him. She'd said she'd call him later, but Doug is irritatingly chill about things. To him, later could mean a day or a week. She'd lied when she'd said Doug was her boyfriend. She doesn't even want him to be. They are whatever they are to one another. Doug would be worried if he knew she was stuck in the elevator, though. She is sure of it.

"Were you pretending like you didn't know me?" she asks Brooks after some thin silence.

"Pretending like I didn't know you? Wow,

really? You think that little of me, huh?" Brooks answers. He is sitting in the corner of the elevator, cattywampus to her, his legs stretched out.

"I don't know," Sierra says, laughs a little. Nervous. She doesn't want to talk to him, but also, she wants to talk to him. Who knows how long they'll be trapped in there and thinking of the word *trapped* makes her feel on the verge of a panic attack. Water usually helps. She feels for her water bottle in her purse and gets it out. Chugs some. Lukewarm and plasticky, but it roots her quickly. "I don't know! Seemed like it," she says as friendly as barbed wire.

"Sierra, I wasn't paying attention. I was busy looking at my phone," he says.

Hearing her name in his mouth again makes her feel drunk. Five tequila shots deep.

"You're still a fancy lawyer?"

"Mmm-hmm, I'm still a *lawyer,* yes," he says.

"Right. Okay." Sierra nods.

Big shot. He will pretend like he doesn't remember what happened at her apartment. When they lay down on the floor together underneath her Christmas tree and looked up.

■ ■ ■

"Did you come over here thinking you'd get laid?" she'd asked him as they sat on her couch, sharing the last of her whiskey from a small glass.

"No, Sierra, I did not. You always say the craziest shit to me, by the way," Brooks said, throwing his head back and laughing. He held his stomach.

"It wasn't *that* funny," she said.

"You're bonkers."

"*You're* bonkers," she said, taking the whiskey from him.

"Are you still dating that . . . guy?"

"I'm always dating some guy."

"I guess I'm always dating some girl too," he said. He leaned against the armrest, made himself even more comfortable.

"I used to be obsessed with you. *Obsessed.*"

"You were not."

"I was! When I was in high school. When I was a freshman. You and Tyler were seniors," she said. Her brother, Tyler, and Brooks had an extreme best friendship. Spending the night with one another every-singleweekend, alternating between their houses.

"You were not *obsessed* with me. You throw that word out there, but that's not the word you mean," he said.

"How are you trying to tell me how I felt? I was obsessed with you! I *was!*" Sierra said. She finished the whiskey and put the empty glass on the floor, tucked her feet underneath her. There was music playing: a folksy Christmas playlist. She didn't recognize any of the artists and she loved it. Everything happening in the moment was new. *Brand* new.

"Ah. You were too young for me anyway."

"No shit, I used to write fanfic about you. I made up stories where we would make out and you'd tell me you loved me," she said.

"Sierra!" Brooks said so bright and sweet, Sierra could taste it.

"Sierra, I wasn't ignoring you. I promise," Brooks says from his elevator corner.

"Whatever."

"What can I say to get you to believe me?"

"I don't know. Nothing, I guess."

"Well, thanks for your honesty," Brooks says. He pulls his phone out and sighs before putting it away again. Sierra feels guilty for being so rude, but doesn't apologize. Can't and won't.

227

"You're welcome?"

"I know who you are," he says. "Trust me."

Sierra and Brooks got a little drunk together by that Christmas tree in her apartment even though all they did was share a small glass of whiskey. For her, some of it was the leftover alcohol in her system and some of it was desire. She didn't know what it was for him, although she hoped at least *some* of it was desire. Lust. The guy she'd been dating had broken up with her recently, but she hadn't told anyone yet. Not even her best friend.

They lay on the floor underneath the Christmas tree, looking up.

"Used to do this all the time when I was a kid, pretend like I was in a rocket ship," Brooks said after a minute or two of not saying anything. The music was still playing. Some brushy acoustic cover of "What Child Is This?" The Christmas songs written in minor keys were Sierra's favorites.

"Same," she said, turning to him. It would be a perfect time for him to finally kiss her, so she told him that.

"Right. And I know who you are too. Brooks Clark, West High class of '05. Homecoming king junior *and* senior year." Sierra starts counting them off on her fingers. "Football dude, ladies' man, and yeah, um, you drove that black sports car your dad got for you the day you turned eighteen. It was all murdered out and you kept it annoyingly clean like it was the only thing that mattered to you in the world. You and Tyler would always take your car to Taco Bell after the football games and hang out in the parking lot so the popular girls would hover around y'all like vultures," she ends and puts her hands back down.

"Wow, okay. Well, I did love that car. That, you are right about," he says.

"I'm right about the other things too," Sierra says confidently. There is a mechanical whirring and the emergency lights flash off and on again. The speaker voice clicks on.

"Are you two doing all right?"

"You could say so. How's it looking?" Brooks says calmly. Sierra is grossed out and turned on by how he says it, by how quickly he takes control. It's sexgusting. That's what she and her best friend call something or someone they're attracted to when they don't want to be. *Sexgusting.* Brooks has crossed his ankles and folded his hands across his stomach like they are resting on a boat somewhere or in a park after a wine and cheese picnic.

"We're almost there. Thanks for your patience. Hang tight," the voice says.

"How long has it been?" Sierra asks Brooks when the speaker voice is gone.

"About fifteen minutes," Brooks says, flicking his phone on and off.

"What happened to your precious car?"

"Totaled it when I was in college. Walked away on angel's wings," he says. "I got another one exactly like it."

Sierra quickly remembers Tyler telling her about the accident, but that must've been after the Christmas-tree night. She'd only seen Brooks a few times since the Christmas-tree night eight years ago and those few times were horrible, awkward nightmares. She's only been dating Doug for a couple weeks but she wonders if Brooks goes to NightVision shows. Good thing she's never seen him at one, since seeing him brings up so much. A lot.

She'd liked that car, although she'd always pretended to ignore it when it was parked in their driveway. Always looked away before Tyler shut its glossy beetle-black doors and came inside.

"Hey, Sierra . . . I miss Tyler. Like, I *really* miss Tyler. Tyler was my brother too . . . my boy," Brooks says, his voice wobbly.

Sierra looks away when her own tears fall.

"I can't kiss you. I'm sorry," Brooks said under the Christmas tree. He slid himself out and sat up.

"Oh," Sierra said, wanting to die of embarrassment.

"Maybe I shouldn't have come over."

"Yeah, maybe you shouldn't have."

"I'll go. But it's not because I don't find you attractive. I mean, you know that, right? You're very pretty. I like looking at you. Always have," he said.

"Okay?" she said, annoyed.

"I'm good to drive. Thanks for having me, Sierra. And I'll see you around. I'd like to see you around."

"Yep. Goodbye, Brooks."

She didn't want to see him around. She never wanted to see him again. She wanted him to disappear. *She* wanted to disappear. She locked the door behind him and lay in bed for hours, hot and embarrassed, not able to sleep until she was pulled completely under against her will.

"Do you know why I didn't kiss you that night? That Christmas-tree night?" Brooks asks.

Sierra is wiping away her tears and thinking of her brother, her big brother. She is still grieving. Everyone in her family is still grieving. Clearly, Brooks is still grieving too. Her parents hadn't had a funeral or a memorial service. Brooks had come by their house several times, bringing flowers and a card. One time, a casserole his mom had made. Brooks kept in touch with her parents. Brooks had been with Tyler the completely normal night before Tyler hanged himself, because being shocking was Tyler's thing. He did whatever he wanted, whenever he wanted.

"No. I don't know why you didn't kiss me that night, Brooks, and I guess it doesn't matter now, does it?"

Sierra gasps when the elevator rattles and jumps. The lights flicker.

Brooks sniffs and she looks at him. He is beautiful in the harsh emergency lights. He smooths his tie.

"When we were kids I swore to Tyler . . . *swore* I'd never mess around with his sister," he says.

Sierra feels cool all over, like someone has opened a winter window in the stuffy elevator.

"Are you serious?" she asks, thinking about it, not super-surprised at Tyler's intensity. It's who he was.

"Swear," Brooks holds up his hand in promise. "Are *you* serious? He was *hella* protective of you. His baby sister? He reminded us regularly that you were completely off-limits. No exceptions."

"And that's it? That's why I've been feeling like an idiot for like . . . *eight* years?"

"You're not an idiot," he says.

Sierra leans her head back and laughs.

"Won't be long now, you two. Still holding up? Not freaking out?" the speaker voice clicks on and asks.

"We're fine," Brooks says.

Sierra laughs some more.

"Sound good enough since you're laughing. Would you like us to leave it stuck for a bit longer, maybe?" the speaker voice asks.

"Ha! Ha!" Sierra says, exaggerating.

"Five minutes," the speaker voice says. The elevator rattles.

"I always wanted to kiss you. *Always,*" Brooks says to her.

Sierra is looking over at him and takes a deep breath. Brooks inches closer to her. Closer. And when he asks permission and leans over to kiss her for the first time, something crooked in the universe is finally fixed. The elevator rattles once again —

shivers for a split second as it powers up and begins its descent.

CREPUSCULAR

The curtain separating my real life from my daydream life was as thin as Bible paper, almost like I could hear the *shh-crinkle* when I pulled it back. My real life was coffee, traffic, work, dinner, drinks, TV, sleep. My daydream life revolved around Abe Forrest, wildlife biologist and host of my favorite nature documentary show, *Forrest Ranger*. I watched it every night before bed and I loved him. I was enraptured by everything he did — how he moved, his white work truck, his hands touching things. I dreamt of morning mimosas with Abe Forrest, lunch with Abe Forrest, dinner with Abe Forrest, bed and life with Abe Forrest. *Abraham.* He tagged and tracked animals like deer and coywolves. He looked at me through my television and said words like *crepuscular* and *wilderness* and *predator*. Sometimes I talked back.

I love you, Abe Forrest. Marry me, Abe Forrest.

I got his email address from the website and sent him a something and practically nothing email.

Abe. Abraham. I'm Lacey. I don't know what crepuscular means and I don't want to look it up. I want you to tell me. I only want to hear it from you. It's more special. So do it. Go on. Tell me.

Two days later he wrote me back. Frisson sparked my shoulders and warmed my cheeks, the top of my head. I got the email when I was at work, so I left my desk and went to the bathroom to read it on my phone.

Hi Lacey. I talked about it in more detail in another episode, but simply put, crepuscular refers to an animal that is active primarily at dusk/twilight and dawn/early morning — an animal that is most active on the edges, when the day pages are turning. Thanks so much for your question and for watching. Best, Abe.

I replied. Three words. Made it holy.

Are you crepuscular?

Sent.

And two more words in my follow-up email: *I am.*

That night, Abe's show was a rerun. He

was discussing coywolves and he used words like *coyote* and *bones* and *feast* and *young*. I sat there on my bed in my long-sleeved *Forrest Ranger* shirt and flowery underwear, watching him. He was wearing the army-green pocket T-shirt he always wore, the same chunky black watch. No wedding ring. I loved his hands and his fingers. I loved his short fingernails, each with their own little pale crescent moon. I watched his arms, his hands as he lifted the tranquilized coywolf pup, as he gently tagged its ear and placed it back into the little dirt hole he'd pulled it out of. "This way we'll be able to track its growth," he said quietly, as if he didn't want to wake a sleeping baby. He was on one knee saying the word *hybrid* when my phone buzzed with his email reply.

Ha! Yes, I am crepuscular too.

Abe was talking and talking, his voice coming from my television as I typed out: *We should be crepuscular together sometime. Love, Lacey.*

I wondered if he'd notice the *Love*. It was true. I loved his compass, his Leatherman, his Swiss Army knife, his headlamp and folding saw. His brown cargo pants, how careful he was around the sleeping baby animals. How wide-eyed he got when he stumbled upon something unexpected. Abe

237

Forrest was my magnetic north. Once he was tagging a tiny fawn and he said look at how small and beautiful she is, she has the prettiest markings. He bent down and said hey there girl in his scratchy, sleepy morning voice. And I wished his voice and those words were crackers so I could eat them. I attached my favorite picture of me to the email, the picture where I'm wearing a white triangle bikini and sunglasses and my hair is all wild and wavy with weather. I was on my brother's boat, eating a peach. It was taken last summer and I wanted Abe to know what I looked like, that I wasn't a dude or a kid. I wanted him to think I was pretty, but, even if he didn't, he'd still like the picture. Maybe it would remind him of a fun summer he'd had on a boat once or a happy, sexy beer commercial or something.

Is this really you? he wrote back.

Yes.

Where do you live, Lacey?

About forty-five minutes from you.

How do you know where I live, Lacey?

I know because I Googled it.

And I had. I'd even written down his address on a torn piece of paper and slipped it into my wallet where I kept the cash. I drew a little heart next to *Abraham* and a little tree next to *Forrest.* I kissed it and left a sticky-cherry lipstick mark. He lived on a street called Halcyon and it felt like a sign. Halcyons were a kind of bird, and his new bird episode was coming on the next week.

It was time for bed, so I turned the TV off and waited for his reply. It wasn't as quick as the others, but it came. Finally.

Well, you certainly are easy on the eyes, he wrote.

I heard his voice in my head saying it, and this too: *Look at how small and beautiful she is, she has the prettiest markings.* I pictured him gently lifting me from my bed, tagging my ear, tracking me all month. A year, maybe.

Abe Forrest came to my house at dusk, two weeks later. He apologized for not being able to make it sooner, but he was traveling, working. When he showed up, he wasn't wearing his work clothes. He was wearing a thin blue-gray plaid shirt rolled up at the sleeves and dark jeans, brown boots. I was wearing a dress and he said maybe he should've worn a tie. I told him no. I told him ties were just penis arrows.

"These men are walking around everywhere with arrows pointing straight down to their penises and they know exactly what they're doing. They do it on purpose, but . . . they act like we don't know . . . ," I said, rambling. Abe laughed. I'd never heard his laugh before. He never laughed on his show. His laugh was husky and if it were a color it would be melon-orange. I loved how his forty-something-year-old eyes crinkled at the corners.

My dress had a belt. I never wore dresses. I got that dress for Abe because I was adorning myself the same way the birds did. *Male bowerbirds decorate their nests with trinkets all the same color to impress their mate.* My dress was blue, my jewelry too — turquoise thunderbird earrings and a bracelet to match, some crystal-blue rings. I poured the wine from a blue bottle into a blue glass. I'd turned on Joni Mitchell's *Blue* album before he got there. "Carey" was coming so soft and low from the speakers we could barely hear it. I put blue corn chips and blueberries on a bright blue plate for him.

"There aren't many naturally blue foods," I said.

"I'm not very hungry, so this is fine. Impressive, actually."

"I'm a bowerbird."

"Oh, I *see*," he said, nodding. His voice, flashlight-bright.

I asked him the scientific name for bower-

240

bird. He said *Ptilonorhynchidae* and it felt like a kiss. I crossed my legs, squeezed my thighs together.

"It's okay if you think I'm crazy."

"I don't think you're crazy."

"But it's totally okay if you do," I said.

"Well, I don't."

I told him he couldn't leave until the morning because we were crepuscular, remember? Since he came over at dusk, he couldn't leave until dawn. I told him nothing had to happen. It was okay if it did, but it didn't have to. I told him men were lucky because they didn't have to be scared when a woman got obsessed with them and looked up where they lived and invited them to their house. Men didn't have to be afraid of women the same way women had to be afraid of men.

"I understand. But you invited me over here and you weren't afraid of me," he said.

"No, but I watch you on TV every night. It's different," I said, smacking more wine into our glasses.

I told him he could sleep on the couch if he wanted. I told him I had a blue blanket.

"And there's something else I want," I said.

"Okay," he said. And I loved that he didn't ask what it was, he just said okay. Joni

Mitchell was still singing because the album was on repeat and Abe and I were drinking and drinking wine, eating and eating chips and berries.

"I want you to talk about me like I'm one of the animals. Y'know . . . follow me around and talk about what I'm doing," I said.

He pulled his phone from his pocket and at first I thought maybe he was calling the police because he was convinced I was a complete maniac, but he held up his phone to record a video, and said okay go.

I picked up the empty blue plate and walked to put it in the sink. I ran some water over it.

"Look. The female bird is cleaning her nest. She is a rare Lacey bird only seen in the western part of the state," Abe said, using his deep documentary narration voice.

My face was hot, my eyes watered. I took my hair down.

"It seems as though she is finished hunting for the night. She's fluffing herself," he said, smiling at me.

I undid my belt. The big horned buckle thunked to the kitchen floor. I looked down, let my hair fall and cover one of my eyes.

"No, wait! Maybe she *is* still hunting . . . looking for a mate. If there are any male

242

birds in the area she will know it very soon," Abe said. He aimed his phone with one hand and leaned against the doorway, stuck his free thumb through his belt loop. He whistled — four snappy, high chirps. I fluffed and fluffed.

STAY AND STAY AND STAY

HOTEL INFORMATION:
Goldenrod Inn & Suites
1616 Ridge Pkwy
Lexington, Kentucky 40503

TRAVEL INFORMATION:
Arrival: Thursday, August 8
Departure: Friday, August 9
Number of Nights: 1
1 Room(s)
2 Adult(s) per room

ROOM INFORMATION:
Room 1 Confirmation Number: 89483028
Guest: You & _____

2-Room Suite with 1 King Bed Nonsmoking (NKS): This deluxe nonsmoking two-room suite features plenty of room for you and your high school biology teacher, Coach Cahill. He's still ten years older, but not twenty-seven to your seventeen — thirty-nine to your twenty-nine. It was winter when you saw him lonely and broken at the bar, like a sturdy table with nicks, now on clearance. Asked him if he'd gotten into a fight with his wife and he didn't answer. You bourbon-and-Christmas-kissed in your car. On the ride home he confessed he'd worn a rubber band around his wrist when you were in high school, snapped it when he thought about you. Bruised and red-sliced his skin for sin. You wanted to lose your virginity to Leonardo DiCaprio until you saw Coach Cahill, then you told your best friend you'd let Coach Cahill take it. (And take it and take it.) You blasted Hole's "Violet" and dressed like Dominique Swain from the *Lolita* movie — milkmaid braids, high-waisted shorts, and saddle shoes. Went to his house on Halloween night and saw his red-haired full-moon pregnant wife in a fuzzy white sweater with a black cat on it. She was handing out little brown and gold foil candy bars and crinkly packages of chalky, pale sweets. She invited you girls around back where Coach Cahill was flannel-shirted, a little beer-buzzed, splitting wood. Your actual virginity wasn't lost in that moment, but it may as well have been. You wanted to slam yourself against the

245

handle of that ax, use his baby-animal-soft shirt to wipe at the sticky blood between your legs. When you used their bathroom you looked at your panties and saw a blood-stain in the shape of Africa, like you had willed yourself to bleed for him. You imagined learning how to navigate the tight hallways of his house in the dark, running your teenage fingers along the nubby walls, feeling for the light switches. In high school he never touched you. Not even once. Not even accidentally. In the suite, there are two spacious rooms separated by a door, but will either of you close it? There is one king bed in the bedroom and a pull-out double sofa sleeper in the living room. *We won't need two beds, but that's the only room they have left. We can leave the couch a couch.* You will want to smoke in here, but you won't do it. The two of you will go out for tacos and beers with limes, buy a hard yellow box of organic cigarettes, go to a dark park and share one. He will say it's not bad for you if you share. You will tell him you made up a new word: *clandestiny.* Secret destiny. The two of you were *clandestined* to be together. You can flick through cable channels you've never heard of on the thirty-seven-inch LCD television while you try to distract yourself from thinking about your boyfriend at home, flossing his teeth, Coach's kids asleep in their brightly colored bedroom, the nightlights glowing their hair. His wife up late watching romantic, foreign movies with her knitting and warm, red wine. You won't use the microwave, iron and ironing board, hairdryer, or coffeemaker. You will use the small humming refrigerator for alcohol and teeth-gritting fruits you won't eat: berries black, straw, and blue. You will not use the phone or the alarm clock. You won't even use the free wireless. You will leave your phone in your bag. You will zip your heart into the mesh pocket of your suitcase, close it so it can hatch new, in reverse — paling from hot-pink to ecru. Sadly, no, you won't be able to sleep in this room. Not after all that sweating. Not after he throws his arm across you while he snores, softly. Satisfied. Before you check out at eleven you will go to the window above the grumbling air-conditioning unit and shove the thick, rough curtains back to look out and see the wet flowers torn up from the hard rain, the strong, short, summernight storm. We will slip the receipt beneath the door and that small flutter will startle you. You will think it's a bird and beware! Birds in rooms are bad luck. Nevertheless, we hope you enjoy your stay! Part of you will. The part that won't? It will not leave you. It will stay and stay and stay.

Room 1 Rate Information

$189.99 per night plus taxes — Starting 08/08

$189.99 USD Total before Taxes*

* Local Taxes will apply.

Two Cherries under a Lavender Moon

The produce section sprinklers hissed on, sending the cool mist into showers across yellow pattypan squash, snake-green zucchini and wild, dirty, white-tasseled scallion ends. Astrid and Henry were standing with their hands gripping their cart handles. This is how they met. It was eleven o'clock at night. They both palmed their three-pound green-globe cabbages. Henry waited patiently as Astrid bagged hers; she moved to the mushrooms as he bagged his.

"The cabbage is on sale. The sign doesn't say it, but if you tell the cashier she'll ring it up for you," Astrid said to Henry over her shoulder.

No one else was in the produce section. Two aisles over, a young man was waxing the floor with a noisy machine.

"Oh! Oh, thank you!" Henry said. Astrid was excited by his excitement and he was a great weirdo to find at night in the produce section.

"I used to boil it, but not anymore. I fry it with bacon or *in* bacon fat, at least. And the purple cabbage doesn't taste the same if you do that. It's too tough. I like to shred the purple cabbage and eat it raw. I make coleslaw with it," Astrid said.

"Coleslaw, all right. Awesome," Henry said, before she knew he was Henry. At that point, she'd decided she was going to call him *Cabbage.*

Astrid saw *Cabbage* in several different aisles before she left the grocery store that night. The first time, she smiled at him again and he did the same. The second time, she smiled at the ground while walking past him. She reached up for the oysters, got two small cans. The third time, she acted like she didn't see him at all.

The following Wednesday, after ballet class and drinks with friends, Astrid stopped by the grocery store, thinking about seeing *Cabbage* again. She'd thought about him in flashes since seeing him the week before. She'd been busy. She'd made enough food so she didn't have to think about what to make for dinner every night — roasted a chicken that would last for two days, used the leftovers in a big pot of white chili. She'd gotten food out with the drinks and friends that Wednesday. Tapas and a strong, minty mojito. She was practically bubbling over as she wheeled her cart to the produce section. And there Henry was, over by the apples. *Apple Henry.* Astrid said hi first.

"Hi. I remember you! Coleslaw!" Henry said. Astrid wondered if that's what he'd been calling her in his mind. *Coleslaw.* She hoped so.

"That's me," Astrid said. Only the two of them in the produce section again. The same young man was waxing the floor with the same noisy machine, this time, three aisles over.

"I made your coleslaw, by the way. I got green cabbage last Wednesday, but then went somewhere else and got purple cabbage and found a recipe on the internet. So technically I guess it wasn't *your* coleslaw, but it was *inspired* by you. Do you mind if I ask your name?" Henry said.

"No. I don't mind," Astrid said.

Henry laughed a little.

"Okay then, I will! What is your name?" he asked, opening his arm across the air like a magician's assistant. She'd already decided she would've let him saw her in half.

"Astrid."

"Henry," he said.

"Hi, Henry."

"Astrid's purple coleslaw," Henry said, almost like he was speaking only to himself.

"Ooh! Sounds psychedelic. I dig it."

"Astrid's purple coleslaw," he said again.

"I'm making zoodles soon. Like, lo mein noodles but zucchini noodles instead. Zoodles," she said, pointing over to the zucchinis.

"Zoodles?" Henry said, guiding his cart over to them.

"I have this thing I hold in my hand and turn . . . makes it into these spirals. Like noodles," Astrid said, miming the movements.

Henry picked up a zucchini like he'd never seen one before. He turned it over in his hands, smelled it. Astrid wondered if she was in love with him. Maybe this was what love felt like. It'd been so long, she barely remembered, but it *did* feel something like this, didn't it? Like watching someone look at something for the first time?

Astrid joined him by the zucchinis and put six of them in a plastic bag, tied it, placed it gently in the top of her cart. She wished she knew Henry better. Wished they'd known one another their whole lives.

Yes, she was sure she was in love with him. This is what it felt like. She wanted to tell him to buy an eggplant. She wanted to see him standing across from her, holding the biggest, darkest-purple, glossiest one.

"You're full of supermarket goodness," he said to her.

"I like how you say supermarket. I say grocery store."

Henry looked at Astrid the same way he looked at the zucchini. She checked his finger for a wedding band. No.

"Let me know how your zoodles turn out," she said. And although she wanted to stand there and talk to him, she also knew how men were. So, she turned away from him and waved without looking back and decided to forego the rest of the produce she needed. She went across the store to the frozen section so she wouldn't accidentally run into him in the other aisles and she breathed a sigh of relief when she didn't.

Because yes. This was definitely love. And to prove it, she got on Facebook that night and happily typed *Henry* into the search bar. She scrolled through a *lot* of Henrys and didn't see a picture of *Cabbage* Henry. Her obsessiveness nipped at her heels before finally sinking its teeth in. Drawing blood.

The next night she cranked Lana Del Rey, put on extra eyeliner, and went to the grocery store just in case. No Henry. But the Lana Del Rey and the extra eyeliner made her feel sexy and powerful. Cool. As cool as the wind on her face as she drove home with the windows down. She was crying her eyeliner off and that was okay because the smudginess made her feel even sexier and more powerful. She mouthed the words after she finished brushing her teeth before bed. *Sexy and powerful.* She let her teeth smooth and catch for too long on her bottom lip. She drifted to sleep imagining herself and Henry out of the grocery store, in the California desert instead. Henry, bearded and Jim Morrison–mysterious, feeding her grapes. The poetry of their tongues. The mouths — two cherries under a lavender moon.

The following Wednesday, after ballet class and drinks with friends, Astrid put on extra eyeliner again and went to the grocery store. Saw Henry in the produce section. She wondered if Henry were a ghost, haunting it. Only on Wednesdays. Like, every Wednesday, no matter what, he would be there in the produce section, waiting for her. Was he even real on the other days? She recognized his back easily now. He was skinny and almost-tall. He was standing there in an expensive-looking navy-blue polo shirt. She touched his shoulder to make sure she couldn't put her hand right through him.

"Astrid the Zoodler!" he said, smiling.

"Henry! I keep finding you here! Here in your supermarket," she said.

"You're a supermarket dream," he said, winking.

"You . . . are," Astrid managed to get out.

"Well, the zoodles were fantastic. Did you think I'd really make them?" he asked.

"Yes. I trusted you."

"What's for dinner this week?"

"How about dessert? Strawberries?" she asked, lifting a big plastic box of organic ones into the air with both hands. She held it over her head, looked at him.

"I love strawberries."

"With . . . chocolate and a light fluffy cake and some whipped cream. Some dark coffee, afterward," she said.

Henry pulled out his phone, started typing.

"I'm writing this down," he said and laughed like he couldn't help it. A cough, really.

"Good boy," she said. She heard the young man two aisles over turn on the noisy machine and begin waxing the floor. "Sailing" by Christopher Cross was piping from the speakers and the produce sprinklers hushed on. Astrid held her pale palm underneath the water.

"Supermarkets and yacht rock seem to go hand in hand," Henry said, looking up.

She nodded. "I came from ballet," she added, liking how it made her seem interesting.

"Do you do ballet to yacht rock?"

"No, I don't," she said, laughing.

"Maybe you should."

"Have a good week, Henry," Astrid said, steering her cart away.

"Hey!" he said behind her.

She turned around.

"You too," he said.

The days in between were becoming painful for Astrid. She wished every day were Wednesday. She found herself checking her phone for texts from him, then remembering he didn't have her number. She didn't even know his last name. She Googled the name *Henry* to see what came up and fell down a rabbit hole of Henry Cavill fan sites, pictures of him in his Superman costume, YouTube clips of his interviews. She found him cloyingly handsome. Saccharine. His jawline, and those perfectly white teeth in a neat row like some kind of fence. He didn't seem real. Not as real as *Cabbage* Henry. She went to bed thinking about him. Woke up wondering if he was thinking about her. Spent Thursday trying to convince herself she wasn't crazy. Spent Friday convincing herself she was.

The next Wednesday night, Henry was in a white T-shirt and jeans and so was Astrid.

"This is embarrassing," Henry said, pointing to himself, then to her.

"You have good taste," she said, smiling.

"What do you have for me this week?" Henry asked. Astrid was sad. This was all they'd ever be. He'd only ask her for recipes, never invite her to eat. He'd never ask her to get a coffee in the little grocery store café or ask for her phone number. Did love feel like this too? Like an empty cup?

"Sweet or savory?" she asked.

"How about this . . . would you like to get a coffee? Over here?" He pointed. "And maybe help me with cheese? I think I want to focus on cheese," he said.

One aisle over, the young man was waxing the floor with the noisy machine.

The light in her heart flickered on, the loneliness scattering to the corners. Yes!

Sometimes love felt like this too — like grocery store coffee. Like cheese and a knife. Maybe. No, yes. Yes, they would most certainly get married in the produce section on a Wednesday night. Astrid, teary-eyed, in her after-ballet clothes, holding a misted bouquet of bok choy and curly kale and rainbow chard. And after Henry put the peach-pit ring on her finger, she would put a cold strawberry in his hand at the exact moment the produce sprinklers turned on. The grocery store manager would click on "Celebration" by Kool & The Gang. The young man would turn off the noisy machine so they could hear the music better. They'd name their baby boy Apricot. Their twin girls, Persimmon and Plum. But, first! Henry and Astrid would get a cake from the bakery and go home together, eat it in bed. Yes, love would sound like "Africa" by Toto, thumping and thumping. Lust was heady at first, but quickly turned bitter and left her thirstier. Ravenous. But, love! Love should feel like being full. Love should feel like, taste like — sweet white buttercream and coconut slathered and tightening all over her like paint, sweet white buttercream and coconut filling her mouth.

WHEN IT GETS WARM

Finding their way through all that winter clothing was as complicated as trying to land a plane in a hurry, Paul joked. Even the mention of flying made Beth anxious. She focused on getting out of her coat and buttons and buttons and zippers and clasps. Her wool sweater, long, soft-flannel sleeves. Once they got down to it, it was blue-ribbon married sex. As comforting as a whistling teapot, the smell of a hardware store. Cinnamon rolls on Christmas morning.

After, Paul went out for some real food. Their plan was to eat the sushi in their room, in secret. Clean and sneak the empty plastic boxes back home in their flowered luggage so the nice woman who owned the B&B wouldn't be offended. Paul had gone to Whole Foods for spicy tuna and ebi, little packages of electric-green wasabi, slivers of tacky, pickled ginger.

Beth was alone in the room. She eyed

Paul's copy of *From Russia with Love* on the nightstand and picked it up, read a bit. Made sure to put the bookmark exactly where he'd left it. She looked through her suitcase, wondering if she'd packed a ribbon. The woman in the book was in bed wearing nothing but a black velvet ribbon around her neck. Maybe she could do that later. Paul loved surprises, especially ones that began or ended with her naked.

He'd been gone for an hour, when it should've taken fifteen minutes. The roads were no doubt freezing over. She called his phone, no answer. She threw on a cardigan and went downstairs, made small talk with Martha, the nice woman who owned the B&B. Martha offered her hot chocolate with marshmallows. Beth took it. Martha pointed toward the glossy magazines fanned in the middle of the coffee table, but Beth didn't feel like reading. She was busy considering life without Paul.

Maybe he'd gotten into an accident, was somewhere dying in the snow, his last gasping breaths smoke-puffing out into the fucking depressing black nothingness of a January night. She checked her phone for the weather, saw it was five degrees. *Five.* She tried calling Paul again, no answer. Sent him two texts:

why is it taking you so long i'm worried about you
it's so cold, i love you

Beth imagined their boys growing up without a father. How could she do this to them? Have them? Bring them into this awful world where their mother or father could die at any moment and leave them alone? The monster of a panic attack gripped her shoulders, opened its mouth to devour her.

She closed her eyes and prayed, begged God to calm her down. *Relax, relax,* she thought, matching her heartbeat-thumps. She drank her hot chocolate. Walked over to the front windows to look out. Nothing. Cars sleeping in the parking lot. Snow and ice.

Martha asked where her husband went. Beth lied and told her he'd gone out for juice.

"Oh, he shouldn't have done that. We have plenty of juice here," Martha said.

"We didn't want to bother you," Beth said, smiling as much as she could.

"Well, if you want anything else please come down and ask me. It's my job and I enjoy it," Martha said.

"Thank you. The hot chocolate is really good." Beth nodded.

She wouldn't feel right wearing bright

261

colors for at least a year after Paul's funeral. No thin, dandelion-yellow vintage summer dresses; no grosgrain carrot-orange ribbons in her hair. Grief was a foggy liver-color seen through a glass, darkly.

Beth started to cry but didn't want Martha to see her, so she took her hot chocolate and headed for the stairs. She'd try to call Paul again. If he wasn't back soon she'd call the police, call her mother. Ask someone if she could borrow their car and go looking for him herself.

She heard the bell tinkle against the door and turned to see Paul in his hat, his puffed black jacket and red-laced hiking boots. He was holding a brown paper bag by the handles. It crinkled. He smiled up at her, stomped off snow.

BOY SMOKE

My big sister, Tula, says her boyfriend, Finn, and his best friend, Kahlil, want us to go for a ride with them. I have a secret crush on Finn. Finn is a senior and quarterback-tall. He got suspended from the football team last week — weed and four Ds on his report card. His dad is the pastor of our church. Whenever I smell communion wafers and baptism pools, I think of Finnegan Grand.

"Kahlil likes you. That's why he wants you to come with us," Tula says. We're at the end of our driveway waiting for the boys to pick us up. She puts on sugar-raspberry lipgloss and hands it to me so I can put it on too.

"He's a'ight," I say after I rub my lips together.

"Here they come," she says, looking down the road.

Kahlil drives a dark green four-door

263

wagon and stops it in front of our house so we can get in the back. He and Finn turn around and say hey. Finn reaches back and holds Tula's hand for a second. I stare at the side of Kahlil's face to see if I can tell if he likes me or not. I come up empty.

Finn wants to ride past Coach Cahill's house. They promise they aren't going to *do* anything to it.

"I'm in enough trouble with my parents," he says, lighting a cigarette and rolling down the window.

"And if we egged his shit, he'd know it was us anyway," Kahlil adds.

"Ruby, do you smoke?" Kahlil asks me.

"Cigarettes?" I ask, all flirty, hoping it will ricochet and wound Finn with bloody love for me.

"She's never smoked anything," Tula says, splitting her hair and pulling it to make her ponytail tighter. Finn hands her his cigarette.

"That's cool," Finn says, turning to smile at me through the tiny crack between the headrest and the car door. I want the sharp, dark tobacco taste of his mouth; I want to sleep in his soft T-shirts like Tula does. He gave her a pearl ring she only takes off for tennis practice. That's when I put it on, pretend like he gave it to me.

Coach Cahill's front door is wide open and Kahlil slows down. Finn tells him to stop.

"What the?" Kahlil says.

The porch bulb casts spaceship-light on the night grass. Coach is gathering a pile of clothes in his arms.

"Damn. His wife is throwing *all* his shit out," Finn says, opening his door.

Coach's wife comes outside. She has a baby on her hip. I get a hot, itchy feeling in my gut thinking about how scared that baby must be.

"Go back in the house!" Coach hollers to her.

"You can't tell me shit anymore!" his wife hollers back.

"Coach?" Finn says, standing in the swimmy milk of the headlights.

I look over at Tula, watch her toss the cigarette. I chew on my thumb.

"What are you doing here?" Coach asks Finn. Coach's shadowed shoulders droop in embarrassment like a robot powering down.

Kahlil kills the engine and lights, gets out of the car. The boys bend, start picking up stuff in the yard.

Coach's wife walks over to us. She leans her head through the driver's side window.

"You girls shouldn't be here," she says like a mom.

"I'm sorry," I say.

"We just came out for a ride," Tula says.

"I don't know what to do," his wife says, shaking her head. Her face looks like a country song: smudged black eyeliner, red wine teeth.

"Do you want a cigarette? We can hold the baby in here so y'know . . . he doesn't smell the smoke," Tula says, pointing to Finn's pack of cigarettes on the passenger seat.

Coach's wife reaches in and gets one. Tula opens her door and holds her arms out for the baby. She puts him on her lap, gently pets his head. I smile at him, let him grab my fingers.

"What are your names?" I ask.

"He's Max and I'm Nina," Coach's wife says, snapping to normal in the way that only women can when they're holding up the Earth. Nina says thanks to us and smokes at the front of the car, standing there like a crownless queen in streetlamp light. We watch the boys clean up the yard. They look like animals.

266

Dandelion Light

Your eyes are two different colors. Heterochromia, you tell me. I tell you I like that word and you ask what other words I like. Cartographer, I say. And I tell you I can draw a map to you. There are a lot of men here and I can drink wine, I say when you ask me what I am talking about, what I am doing. I put my glass on the table and take a pen from my purse, grab a stiff hay-colored cocktail napkin from the top of the stack. I draw a small skull and crossbones, a fat heart, the outline of Kentucky — a crazy jagged, pointed elf's shoe with no foot. You ask me what it means and I tell you I forgot the X so I draw it. Write YOU ARE HERE underneath. I cross everything out one by one and throw the napkin away after I kiss it and finish the rest of my wine. You are slightly buzzed. I can tell by the way you don't shake your head when you tell me I am a piece of work. And the *c* sound in the word *piece* doesn't snake out as slick as it should. It sounds like your tongue tripped and stumbled out of a thick, rustling bush at night with its eyes closed, its hands straight out in front of it, feeling for anything.

We've met before. No one is surprised when we leave the party together and walk and walk and walk. The neighborhood smells like everyone's laundry and dinner. I have terrible allergies. I even moved to Arizona to try to fix them, but it didn't work, I say. Our arms reek of peppery-lemon citronella, stolen sprays from the bottle of DEET-free bug repellent by the back door. This neighborhood is rife with mosquitoes, I warned you. And I know where we are going. I am leading you to wet grasses and backyard clover. We lie watching the evening clouds and listening as if we can hear them click into place, watch the curved world shift from simmering-sunset light to firefly light. Moonlight, starlight when you devour me like I am a sweet, little cake — worship me like I am a cooling token in your hot-hot hand or a prehistoric translucent-winged insect in a perfect square of warm, clear amber. Something you could slip a string through and wear around your neck for good luck. Tonight I am your amulet, the bundle of snapped branches long burned white.

Our first official date isn't even a date, it's a science experiment, you say when you're as sober as a kitten. We fell asleep in the vegetable garden. I don't know what time it is and I don't care. I tell you I hate science and shrug when you ask if you can see me again. Smile when I say stay here because you are seeing me now. You are slipping a flower behind my ear when I tell you I'm hungry. We go inside my house, clatter in the kitchen. I pull a white paper box of chicken from the refrigerator. I wilt spinach and green onions in a cast-iron skillet. We sit across from one another, under the gauzy-white low-hanging kitchen table light. We clink and drink unsweetened iced tea with the little lemon bars I made the night before. Baking as therapy, I say. I tell you that a year ago, my husband and I moved back to Kentucky from Arizona and got a divorce and now, he already has a new wife and our twin daughters are with them for the weekend. I tell you my daughters' hair is like blackbird feathers and I hook my thumbs to make bird wings with my hands. How am I drunk when I only had one glass of wine? I laugh but we both know I am not drunk, I am sad. And tonight those words can mean the same thing. So can *man* and *friend. Kiss* and *talk*. We use our mouths and tongues for both of them, don't we?

Your phone rings and I'm sure it's your wife. Sure you've been lying about everything. You answer and I turn away from you, an attempt at gifting you a private moment. I get up from the table, take our dishes to the sink, wash them by hand. The faucet water sounds like rain.

It's your daughter. She needs a ride. She got in a fight with her mom. You say they do this all the time . . . this is what they do . . . I better go get her . . . they always end up scratching each other. You make a small claw with your hand, scratch at the air. You tell me you were never married. You tell me your daughter is *very thirteen*. You slip your phone back into your pocket when you say it, slip your hand in too. I tell you I understand . . . my daughters are *very eleven*. I say you can drive my car and when we get downtown, the sun is coming up. Your daughter has been crying and her long, wet eyelashes are black butterfly wings behind the slight lens magnification of her thickish red-framed glasses. She is beautiful and short and brown. Zaftig. You tell her I'm your friend, I let you drive my car. You drive it to your place and when we go inside you make a big pot of coffee. I drink it black out of an auto body shop mug. I never drink it black, but I don't want to bother you by mentioning soy milk and stevia because you don't seem like the kind of guy who has heard of either and I like that. You point at the mug and tell me you used to work there. I look closely at the design and see your name at the bottom written in white cursive. Above it, there is a drawing of a half-naked woman with huge pointy tits. She is resting on the crushed bumper of a broken car. It's so stupid it makes me laugh and makes you laugh too. Your daughter comes out of the bathroom and says she's going to bed but then she asks what's so funny. We try to explain, but it's not funny anymore. Our laughter swings down slowly, reverses itself back into our mouths. You hug her and kiss her head and I tell her goodbye, that I hope I see her again soon. Maybe. I tell her how much I like you and the confession feels like an accident. Like stubbing my toe.

I finally walk onto the porch to leave and you hold the mug out for me. Tell me to keep it. I hug it to my chest like it's a baby animal. You ask if you can kiss me and I say why do men ask — either do it or don't. And you say you are a gentleman, that you are only being polite and I say we've already kissed and like, done things, so I don't know if it counts anymore. I whisper yes, gentleman, please kiss me. You do. You kiss me with the deliberateness of carefully pouring acid from one beaker to another — the slightest mistake and we could have a Situation. This chirping summer morning, ever so surely our catalyst.

When I get home I text, *hey you left your socks.* You write me back, *wow I didn't realize I took them off* and ask if you can call me later. I write, *yes, gentleman.* I tell you I will take off all of my clothes and put on your striped socks and sleep in them to keep them warm. You send me a word you like: *erstwhile.* I send you *summer afternoon.*

Cellar door.

Dandelion light.

California, Keep Us

Marco had this idea that twelve times a year, we go away. We leave here. We don't tell anyone what we're doing or where we're going — it's no one else's business. The first time? He'd mailed a typewritten letter to our house. It'd gotten here on the first day of his business trip. Marco is a very capable man, rational, a planner. He'd flown from Kentucky to LA. I hadn't expected to see him until after the weekend and I was busy too. His letter was addressed to *Miss K. Huff, traveling.* He'd used my maiden name. Inside the envelope was a plane ticket and a letter:

BOUGAINVILLEA, BUNGALOW
UPCOMING FRIDAY BEFORE DINNER
UNTIL SUNDAY AFTER BREAKFAST
x
M(arco)
PS: DON'T TELL ANYONE. THIS IS FOR

ONLY US. TAKE THE TICKET. COME TO LOS ANGELES. I WILL PICK YOU UP @ LAX. I LOVE YOU. I LOVE YOU.

Our baby was Bougainvillea. I hadn't named her; she'd named herself. She'd told me her name in a psychedelic purple vision-dream the night before I bled and lost her. Six months afterward, I told Marco I wanted to have an affair. I didn't tell him this on purpose to hurt him. I was in a fugue state. Looking at Marco's face meant looking into the face of the baby girl we had to bury. I didn't want to look at Marco's face anymore, but I couldn't look away. I'd loved Marco's face since I was a little girl. We met in elementary school. *Marco Hernandez. Kendall Huff.* He always sat right in front of me. I looked at the back of his head for twelve years before we were a couple.

Bougainvillea, Bungalow meant the place Marco had rented for us in California. It took me about four hours to fly there alone. I kept my promise and didn't tell anyone. That part wasn't hard. When our baby Bougainvillea died, I stopped talking to people as much. I didn't have anything to say. And the way I'd previously withstood small talk although I hated it with the fire of a trillion suns? That went away too, a relief. I didn't have to pretend anymore. I allowed myself to be as selfish as I wanted to be, and Marco did too. Our baby was born dead. We deserved quiet. We'd earned it. Marco and I would be in our house together, our home, and sometimes we wouldn't say a word to one another. We lived like this for months. But sometimes, we talked about B and that's what we started calling her anyway. B. *Bee.* It made it easier because we could imagine she wasn't a real human we could lose. Not then, not ever. She was something else completely. *A bee.*

Marco told me I didn't want to have an affair, I just wanted to feel better. We were sad together all the time, trapped in the same smothering grief coat. I asked Marco if he wanted to have an affair and he said yes and no. He said he wanted to have an affair with me. He said we could pretend to be other people because it was what people did when they experienced trauma. He told me we'd experienced trauma. And I hated assigning that word to myself, even though it was true. Trauma sounded a whole lot like something you couldn't come back from. Like *terminal* and *eternity.*

I apologized to Marco for saying I wanted to have an affair. It wasn't what I meant. I'd never been with anyone else and I didn't want to be. I just wanted to feel better. I wanted to go back to a place and time where I wasn't a mother without a baby, an oyster shell with no pearl. A place and time before I hadn't been able to hold on to our *Bee.* A honeycomb with no honey. Marco got deliriously angry whenever I blamed myself for losing her. One night I was crying and wouldn't stop saying it. The was the night I said I wanted to have an affair. The following day, Marco sent me the invitation. *Bougainvillea, Bungalow.* And I flew to California to meet M.

He'd texted me and asked me to wear a dress. I'd gotten a dovegray dress and put it over black leggings. I was wearing some strappy gold sandals and a medium-sized pair of gold hoop earrings. The dress was comfortable, not sexy. I started crying about it as soon as I got into the deeply air-conditioned rental car Marco was sitting in. He was quiet and drove away from the airport until he could pull aside safely. He turned the car off and looked at me.

"I'm sorry my dress is so plain."

"You look beautiful. And everything is different out here. We can be whoever we want to be out here. We don't have to grieve here,

Kendall. We have a weekend. *One* weekend a month when we can pretend." He held up his finger.

His clothes were new and my blood flashed thinking of him going shopping alone, picking out something just for me, just for the weekend. It wasn't something Marco would usually do, but this wasn't Marco, this was M.

"You look handsome. You bought all new things. I love this," I said, reaching out to touch his new tie, to let my finger slick down. "This dress isn't sexy. I screwed this up already."

M kissed me. M kissed me like he thought my dress was sexy, like we weren't sad at all, like we'd never been sad. M kissed me like our baby had never died, like the letter *B* didn't exist like *bees* didn't exist, like the alphabet went right from *A* to *C* and every flower pollinated itself. Even the bougainvillea. We could start over in California — the oceans, mountains, and trees that didn't stop growing even when they scraped the sky. I kept my eyes closed tight and kissed him back like I was with my husband and having my affair too. *M. Marco.* A familiar mystery. He wrapped his arms around me like I was all he'd ever wanted and now. Now, he finally had it. And when we stopped kissing, he took a deep breath and started the engine again and drove us to the bungalow — the bungalow dripping in bougainvillea. The sun-heat smacking my dusky skin and his too as he lifted my luggage from the back of the car and carried it inside.

M was completely different from Marco in bed. Marco was quiet and focused, tender. Sweet. M was sexy-rough and vocal about what he wanted, what he liked. I wrapped my legs around M's waist and he held my hands over my head, locked our fingers together. Is this what you wanted? To fuck someone else? To have me fuck you like you're someone else? I don't want someone else. I want you, he said in the deep, breathy voice that only came out when his mouth was warm against my ear, in darkness, in bed. I could see the slinking shadows of our clothes, snaking from the bedroom door to where we lay. M had locked the door behind us and put his hand down my leggings, between my legs and told me I was sexy no matter what I wore. He loosened his tie and asked if it was okay, if I was okay and I nodded against his neck and gasped. Gasplaughed and made a noise I was unaware of until it came out of my mouth. As if a chipmunk or some kind of squeaky animal had leapt from my stomach to my heart, careened between my lips. We stumbled to the bedroom like a four-legged monster, M behind, his finger inside me, his other hand up my shirt. And anytime I thought about our baby I squeezed my eyes together as tightly as I could and told myself I was in California and *we don't talk about death in California.* Everything was different in California. *We* were different in California and I didn't have to think about any of that until Sunday. It was Friday and the air smelled like oranges, like a lemon ocean. I was having an affair with M, secreted away with the flowers.

M went out to get us food, came back with sushi and hot sauces, sticky rice and slippery noodles, crispy noodles, fried egg rolls with cabbage and carrots and shredded pork. He'd put his nice clothes back on and when he returned, he changed into a new pair of white pajama bottoms. The night had turned windows-open-cool. And I told him he'd never smacked my ass hard enough when I asked him to. He surprised me by quickly dropping his chopsticks and scooping me up, putting me on the couch. Taking his time to slowly pull up the hem of my white nightgown, to let his fingers brush my skin before he smacked me. Hard. My eyes stung with tears and I took a slick of breath in.

"How's that?" he asked.

"That's good."

He smacked me. And, again.

"That's good," I repeated.

"I've never done this?" he asked, smacking me again. I arched my back.

"You never want to hurt me."

"No. I don't," he said, rubbing me where he'd smacked. Leaning over and kissing me where he'd smacked. Turning me over and wetting his face, devouring me while our food cooled next to us on the table.

We left California together on Sunday. When we were back home, I called him Marco when I was crying in the bathroom and needed him to bring me more toilet paper.

"And we can't always go to California. It's too far. We can't afford it," I said, sniffing.

"I've already planned it out. Four times a year we do California, the rest of the year we'll go somewhere closer. We *can* afford it. That's not for you to worry about, it's for me to worry about and I'm not worried about it," he said, handing me the roll. I took it. "Listen to me. Kendall, look at me," he said.

I looked at him. I tore off a piece of toilet paper and blew my nose. I was sitting on the edge of the sink in my underwear, crying about our baby. Crying about our life when we *weren't* in California. Every other place in the world had become *not*-California.

"I already know where we're going next month and you'll love it. M will send you a letter like before . . . tell you where. You promise to come?" he said, touching the top of my head, letting his fingers slide down my hair. He held his hand there, holding my braid, the end.

"I promise. I'll finish crying and then I'll come out," I said.

"I love you," he said.

"I love you, too."

He closed the door.

I've caught Marco sobbing in the bathroom several times. It's usually when he's in the shower and he thinks I won't hear him, but I do. And that night, that's what happened. Marco took a shower and sobbed in there like I wouldn't hear him and I acted like I hadn't when he came out of the bathroom. I'd made him dark, hot tea and butter cookies and we sat in the living room together afterward, with woodsy cello suites summoning twilight.

The darkness always came too soon, took me by surprise every evening, as if I were relearning everything like someone who'd been in an awful accident. All three of us had been in an awful, brutal accident. Only Marco and I had survived.

The wild Kentucky moon rose and we stepped outside together to look at it. I put my arms around his waist, his soft college sweatshirt. I was saying *M, we'll keep doing this. I can't wait to get back to California. I want to have a baby girl and name her California,* when the velvet raven mouth of night opened wide and swallowed us up again. Quenchless.

CLOUD REPORT

I remember Bradley's advice about not gripping the armrests so tightly. *Crystal, that's not relaxing,* he'd said quietly and bright blue before smiling over at me the last time we'd flown together. We'd been headed to Chicago to visit his family.

Louisville Muhammad Ali International Airport to O'Hare International Airport. In-air flight time: 51 minutes.

I was newly pregnant with Evan then. That was before we'd moved from Louisville to Atlanta so Bradley could take a better job. Now Evan is three and I am leaving him for the first time. Heather's bridal shower is a week before the wedding and I want to be there for all of it. I am her Best Girl the same way she was mine. Bradley and Evan are flying to Chicago again, to spend time with Bradley's mother, who — finally divorced from Bradley's dickhead father — now happily purchases matching toe ring and ankle bracelet sets. Silver stack-printed rings that say *live laugh love*.

Hartsfield-Jackson Atlanta International Airport to O'Hare International Airport. In-air flight time: 1 hour, 25 minutes.

They'll drive down to meet me in Louisville in a few days. Everything is exciting, I am looking forward to everything, but I have to get through the flight first.

Hartsfield-Jackson Atlanta International Airport to Louisville Muhammad Ali International Airport. In-air flight time: 57 minutes.

I let go of the armrests and touch the cool, gold locket around my neck, the photo of my big sister, Amber, still safe inside. Always. I'd put it on a couple days after she died when I was in high school and rarely took it off. Amber was forever eighteen. I am the oldest now, the only. I am thirty-seven, I am thirty-five thousand feet in the air. The photo of Bradley and Evan on my lock screen, both smiling. Bradley is frozen with one hand shielding his eyes from the sun with Evan on his hip, in his *Captain America* T-shirt. Evan's hand is lifted, stuck in a spread-wide wave. He resembles his daddy incredibly, almost like I'd had nothing to do with it. Like they hadn't needed me. I'd done all the work!

Good thing I love Bradley's face as much

as I do. His calm, brown eyes and bashful smile. How his nose comes to a pert point when it's finished. It's perfect. I love that Bradley has given those things to Evan, our only. And it isn't all lost because Evan has my wild, curly hair, the underneath and edges occasionally burning red in the summer sun.

I'd been careful to pack Evan's bag for Bradley knowing full-well that Bradley would wing things anyway, like he usually did. And I'm trying to relax about that too. I am constantly reminding myself to let go and imagining the successful Velcro-snatch of separating my intrusive worries from my pleasant thoughts. It'll be okay if Evan wears the same pair of shorts two days in a row or if Bradley's mom lets him have two cookies. Three, even! But, I still can't help myself from crying a little when I click on my phone to take a look at the photo again and open my text messages. Bradley had texted me right before takeoff.

Remember the flight is short, only about an hour! You'll be fine! We'll be fine! Have fun! Try not to worry too much! We'll be together soon! We love you!

Bradley had added all the exclamation points for me, to make me feel better. He's a natural-born encourager. I wipe my tears and read his text again and when I consider gripping the armrests one more time, I hear Bradley's voice in my head. *That's not relaxing.* So I take a deep breath and confidently ask for a white wine when the flight attendant steps next to me.

"Actually, I'll have two wines please," I say.

The flight attendant also hands me a small, crinkly package of tissue and winks at me. She's old-Hollywood pretty and I like looking at her.

And with my wines and my book, I'm okay. I'm better. I don't obsessively imagine our plane bursting into flames or exploding into the colored quilt of cornfields and farmland. I don't constantly imagine Bradley putting the yellow oxygen mask on himself first, then slipping it over Evan's tiny head and ears. The gasping. No. Stop.

Stop! I am excited to see Heather. I haven't seen her since Christmas! She'll be a beautiful bride next week, marrying the person she's always been waiting for. Heather and I lost our virginity on the same day in the same house that high school summer with those best-friend boys whose intense relationship mirrored ours. Inseparable, rascally, wild. Heather got her heart broken, but only mildly. Jamie and I had dated for a few months before breaking up and before I moved away, we'd seen each other every now and then at the grocery store, the park. One time at the pediatrician's office, both of us smiling and speaking quietly, rocking our sleeping, feverish babies.

Jamie and I have been friends on Facebook ever since and I didn't hate thinking about that summer afternoon on his best friend Tristan's couch, all those summer afternoons on all those couches. My blood jumps when I think about how maybe I'll run into Jamie when I'm back in town, how he'll always be my forever-first and he's not a half-bad one. Even Bradley has said that my relationship with Jamie is sweet. After Jamie I'd dated a string of assholes until I graduated from college and met Bradley, who I like to say has either burned through his asshole tendencies before meeting me or never had them in the first place, which always makes him smile.

When we were in high school, Heather and I would kiss before we went to sleep at night. Real kisses, with tongue and we never told anyone about it. I think even telling Bradley would be a small crease of betrayal, but I do wonder what he'd think about it if he knew. Although not like we used to,

Heather and I still kiss on the mouth when we see one another, because it's how we've always been. We love each other so much; kissing each other makes sense. We've always been in love with each other and it's different than anything we've ever felt for a man. Not deeper, but . . . *diagonal.*

It took me forever to get pregnant, but Heather had gotten pregnant on accident. I miscarried that baby, Heather had hers and now he's twelve. I was jealous and angry about how easy it'd been for her, but she wasn't happy and her relationship fell apart. I spent years and years trying to get pregnant again; I lost track of how much money we spent. Now, Heather is getting married to a person who actually deserves her, and I have my baby too. There is so much to celebrate! I hold this thought in my head as we soar. Every baby born grew in a woman's womb and planes soar through the sky! Sometimes, everylittlebit of life is full of wonder.

I drink one wine and read my book — comforting, predictable domestic fiction with goodhearted people worth rooting for. I'd purposely avoided bringing along anything too thrilling or anxious, my heart and personality doing enough of that on its own. The cold wine slowly cools my hot, flickering worries.

My sister, Amber, died with her boyfriend and part of it remains a forever mystery. And I think of those two words in *Lolita* describing the freak accident that killed Humbert Humbert's mother, how they're written in parentheses — *(picnic, lightning)*. Amber's accident reads *(car, river)*. My therapist likes to remind me that the trauma of losing my sister when she was a teenager, when I was a teenager, had and will continue to have far-reaching effects, but that doesn't mean my *worst* worries will always come true. I'd never properly worried about something awful happening to Amber. And until it happened, nothing did. And once it did, it was over. There wasn't even time to be scared. No prep work, no anticipation. Just the fallout — the shrapnel and scattered remains of what our family used to be, strewn about — all of us trying our best to be okay.

I am wearing my go-to travel outfit: pointy bright pink flats I ordered online after Oprah mentioned them, a light, long-sleeved tunic and leggings — all things that curb my anxiety and make me feel at home no matter where I am. I rub lavender oil on my wrists and sniff. I put on the expensive citrusy hand lotion Bradley's mom gave me for Christmas. I reapply my tingly lipgloss and consider the hydrating overnight mask in my bag and whether or not I'll remember to put it on after dinner and drinks with Heather. Probably not. I look at my lock screen photo, at my husband and our little boy, the rainbow lens flare in the corner, faking the sun. I pray for them like I always do. My heart — a tight fist.

The man next to me tells me he's excusing himself to the bathroom and I step into the aisle so he can get out. Across from me, a man and woman have just met, but have happily hit it off. She's a musician and the man is already asking her to list off some of her recent albums as he takes dubious notes on his phone. Their bubbly mirth spreads across the aisle to me. It's infectious. Calming. It helps. The bathroom man has left a puzzle piece space between me and who I can only assume is his wife, looking out the window. I tell myself I can look at my lock screen photo one more time before putting it away and once I slip it back into my bag, the woman next to me looks over.

"I couldn't help but notice you looking at the picture of your little boy," she says, sweetly.

"Oh! Yeah. It's my first time away from him. He's three. I'm trying to remain calm about it," I say.

"We just dropped our son off. He's shipping out soon. He can't tell us where he's going. I'm a wreck about it, but I'm trusting he'll be fine. It's all I can do. Trust," she says.

"How old is your son?"

"Eighteen."

"I cried myself to sleep last night because I'm not going to see my son for a few days. I can't imagine dropping him off and not knowing where he's going. That must be so hard. You're strong!" I say.

"I don't feel very strong," she says, sniffing. The package of tissues the flight attendant gave me is sitting in my lap so I hand it to the woman. My wine buzz clicks on, soft.

"Well, you *are* strong. Mamas have to be strong. I'm trying too," I say, laughing through my own tears as she slips a tissue out and hands the package across her husband's empty seat, back to me.

"It's good for your little boy for you to get away . . . for you to take some time to yourself," she says.

"That's what my husband says. My mom too."

"But it's still hard."

"It is," I say.

"What's your little boy's name?" she asks.

"Evan."

"What's your son's name?" I ask.

"Quincy," she says.

"Oh, I love that name."

"I love Evan, too."

We smile and shake our heads at one another, at ourselves, at our airplane tears. Our emotionalism. I want to tell her everything. I want to tell her how strong my own mother is and had to be after losing my sister. I want to tell her how strong Heather is for leaving her abusive relationship and raising her son on her own for so long. I want to hear about the strong women in her life, how we put one foot in front of the other even when it feels like the world's most impossible task. I want to tell her that Amber was a strong woman too, she just hadn't had a chance to keep going. I touch the locket around my neck, double-check that it's properly pressed closed. I look at the woman's profile, the haze and heavenly wonder of both the flat and fluffy clouds outside her window. The horizon, proof of the unfathomable sky.

The woman's husband appears in the aisle beside me and I wipe my nose quickly and move so he can return to his seat. I smile over at the woman and she smiles too, our female secrets like mist, quickly and easily blown away by the mere presence of a man between us. I reach for the armrest, remember Bradley's *that's not relaxing* and let go. I finish my wine, read some more.

Louisville Muhammad Ali International Airport. 85 degrees. Winds 5 mph.

By the time we land I'm a little drunk. I text Bradley that I'm okay, that I made it, that I had wine. I ask if he and Evan are okay.

We're fine! We miss you! Call me in a little bit! Have more wine if you need it!

I smile. All those exclamation points are turning me on. He knows exactly what to do. I love him so much. Oh, how I wish Amber had lived to meet Bradley. They would've loved each other. There isn't a day that goes by that I don't wonder what she'd be like now and think about how much she would love Evan, how much he'd love her.

Before we disembark, the woman by the window takes my hand and squeezes, tells me to enjoy myself. I tell her I'll try my best, I tell her I'll pray for Quincy, wherever he is, wherever he is going. And I pray it right then and there so I won't forget. I'm so thankful Evan isn't old enough to join the military yet, isn't leaving me anytime soon. I still have time. *We* still have time. Anxiety itches at me as I double-check my phone to make sure I'd told my mom and Heather the right time. Maybe I should text them again. But no, I look up and see them. Waiting for me with a little white sign that reads WE LOVE CRYSTAL in fat pink marker. My eyes tear up, my face heats — because I've been thinking about Amber, because I've been so worried, because being a human is hard, because being a mom is hard and because I've missed them both so much.

"Aw, I missed you," my mom says.

"I've missed you too," I say.

"I'm so glad you're here," Heather says.

"I'm so glad to *be* here."

We step out into wisteria-summer air, walking to my mom's car. And before we get in, Heather puts her hands on my cheeks and kisses my mouth. I kiss her back. I feel better. I prayed for Quincy to be okay, for his mom to be okay. Bradley's okay, Evan's okay, I'm okay. I have a pair of shark socks and a Braves cap in my bag for Heather's son for later, a present from me — his Aunt Crystal who loves him so much. It feels good to be home. Small victories! Now this, *this is relaxing.* And Heather's lips still taste like cherries or strawberries or pink or grape or blueberry or lemon or Dr Pepper. Girl-gravity.

Dolly smelled the sea. No. It was *him*. She hated his sexiness. How annoying. There he was smelling clean. Smelling blue. *Celeste.* Smelling like the sky and six sharp hours of puck-white sun. Kent, her husband Jed's new friend from work. Jed had called on his way, asked if it were okay for Kent to come home with him. She'd heard Kent in the background. It was embarrassing. How could she say no? She'd met him a few times before — quick, meaningless. Like two leashed puppies passing on the sidewalk.

In Dolly's kitchen, Kent held out his hand for her to shake.

"Oh," she said with a crinkle of disappointment at his formality. She shook it and smiled.

"My wife Vale is coming by a little later after she drops the kids at her sister's," he said.

Kent reminded her of Jed and that's what was sexy about him. They were both in pressed Oxford shirts and dress pants but she preferred to think of them smoking in dirty Carhartts, bending down and stretching up, fixing broken things. She preferred thinking of Jed as the tobacco farm country boy he was, not the man he'd become. They'd been in love since college, but that didn't keep her from wondering how Kent touched his wife. *Vale.* Dolly had never met Vale and tried to picture what kind of woman Kent would be married to. She knew they had three young sons. Just like that. *One two three.* Dolly and Jed had a ten-year-old girl, a six-year-old boy, and one amethyst-colored betta fish trapped in a glass bowl next to the junk mail on the counter.

Dolly loved Jed and his friend was sexy, that was all. So what. She'd made a cheesy chicken casserole because that's what she was making anyway and didn't change it when Jed called on his way home. Their kids were at sleepovers. Dolly was a little drunk already, on her second glass of wine. She'd just pulled the casserole out of the oven. Kent leaned against the counter. Jed clinked around in the fridge for beers.

"Your sons . . . what are their names?"

she asked Kent and forgot as soon as he said them. There was an M at the beginning of one of them, a Y at the end of another, and one of the names dripped from his mouth and spilled on the floor — never made it to her ears.

The kitchen was torrid. July in the South was ungodly. She fanned herself. The rattle of the amber locusts out back? Apocalyptic. Jed opened Kent's beer and his own and stood next to her, looked over. He pushed away and led Kent to the garage, to show him things.

They were gone. Dolly texted her sister.

what if I left Jed and took the kids and came and stayed with you?

Her sister wrote her back quickly.

WHAT?!

i said WHAT IF. calm down.

Is something going on?!? CALL ME.

i'm fine. i'll call you later. busy right now.

Dolly deleted the messages and turned her phone off.

Kent came back to the kitchen without Jed. Told her Jed had gone to the bathroom.

"How long have y'all lived here?" he asked, looking around.

"I hate small talk. I asked you your boys' names earlier but to be honest, I didn't even listen. I still don't know them. Even if you put a gun in my mouth and threatened to blow my brains out of the back of my head, I couldn't tell you," she said, finishing her wine.

"All right. That's all right," Kent said. A tender cowboy.

"I know it may seem like I'm being rude but it's our house, right?" she said. A tetchy cowgirl.

"Absolutely."

"Jed's taking a shower?" she asked, knowing it already. She heard the water turn on. It annoyed her how he always took a shower when he came home from work, no matter what. He took one in the morning, he took one in the evening. He had no smell. "*I'm* being rude. *He's* being rude. Why did you want to come over here again?"

"You come off like a bitch, but no worries . . . I think you're interesting," Kent said, drinking. Dolly poured more wine, hopped up on the counter.

"Okay, so do you think I'm pretty? I think you're sexy . . . handsome. Isn't this a betrayal to tell you that in my husband's home? Isn't this the *worst* possible thing I can do?" she asked. He stood closer to her and she touched his tie. Slipped it between her fingers as she drank. Her nose inside the glass like that made her feel underwater.

Like she was the one in a fishbowl. She blew tiny bubbles into her wine before putting it down.

"You're pretty."

"Thank you."

"Even prettier than you think you are," he said.

"Fuck off. I think I'm pretty."

"Sure you do." And he winked.

"Everyone lies all the time. No one on this Earth wants to tell or hear the truth anymore," she said. Her eyes filled with tears and she drank again. Finished her glass in a gulp. Drunk drunk drunk. "Don't tell your wife about this. Most people can't handle . . . *anything*." She undid the knots, shoved off a little boat of anger in her heart. Climbed inside, hoisted the sails. Didn't look back.

"Tell her what?" he asked. He was standing so close to her. So close. She spread her legs a bit and he stood in between them. Her stomach, a rabbit. She could feel his breath on her face.

"Any of this," she whispered.

"Any of what?" he whispered back.

The shower was still running — a storm from another room. Rain behind the door.

"Don't tell *him* any of *this*," he said, nodding to the bathroom.

"Any of *what*?"

He rubbed his thumb across her bottom lip. Smushed it to one side, then the other. Did it again. Harder. Smeared her lipstick.

"I don't tell anyone anything," she said, closing her eyes.

"Me either," he said, putting his beer on the counter next to her. The dripping cool of it, wet relief against her thigh.

The shower was still running — a tempest — the shower was still running when Kent slipped his thumb into her mouth.

"Who even *are* you?" he asked and pulled his thumb out, put his hand on the back of her head. She tilted — a crescent moon. She was all lit up like Ursa Major, the *great she-bear.* He kissed her neck.

Dolly looked up at the ceiling before closing her eyes again. *God will hate me for this. God hates sin, but God can't hate me.* She wanted Jed to walk out of the bathroom and catch them. She wanted Vale to come to the back door and press her hands against the screen in order to see them better. She wanted Loretta Lynn to sit at her kitchen table with a guitar and write a three-chord song about this.

Poor Jed turned the shower off. She heard him step out and walk down the hallway to get dressed. He was humming something

300

he made up, nothing she recognized. What was happening was so shocking and fresh, it had her craving something to root her. Something comforting. Familiar. But no. Kent smelled like water and her body was water. There they were being water together. His mouth, a tributary. He kept kissing her. Hummed on her neck. A duet. This buzzing chorus. She was sticky-summer-dizzy and letting herself be awful. Downright lousy.

You Got Me

Lowell called me woman. *Woman, when's the last time you had your oil changed? Woman, have you seen my hat?* I called him Low.

Low had a cowboy heart. I would've married him simply for how his body slicked over when he played pool. The clacking of those pool balls was the soundtrack to our relationship. And how he'd say rack 'em and somehow make it the dirtiest, sweetest thing I'd ever heard.

We knew each other, hung out before. This was different. This time we spent four consecutive, frothy, slippery days together. Late nights hushed into early mornings without either of us noticing. *Woman, I'm fixin' to go to the gas station,* he'd said, putting his hat on. It was Saturday afternoon. He never came back. I didn't call.

Saturday night.

Sunday.

I didn't go to his favorite bar because I knew he'd be there — slicking over, shooting pool. Saying rack 'em to some girl who wasn't me.

Monday.

Tuesday.

I thought about calling him but didn't. I went to work and came home. I had dinner with a man I didn't like. A man who said terribly generic things like: *I love music.* I swear I about had to stop myself from dying right there at the table — from rolling my eyes back as far as they would go, from letting my body slam down as hard as it could and crash-clinking the silverware to the floor.

Wednesday.

Thursday.

I drove past Low's house, saw his truck out front. I didn't slow down. My whole body hurt. I prayed for rain — a purple-blue tempest, lightning slicing sky.

Friday.

I went to The Willow because he'd be there. I got a beer and leaned against the doorway. Watched him. I listened for a screeching feedback sound when he locked eyes with me, like we shouldn't be that close to each other anymore and even the walls of that bar knew it. The fuzzy Hooker's green felt of that pool table knew it. I mouthed *fuck you* slowly, sipped his favorite beer. His face flashed, he raised his eyebrows and put his pool stick down. Told his friends he'd be just a sec.

"Woman, did you cuss me?" he asked, leaning.

"You walked out on me before anything got good and started."

"You're mad I left first? You didn't call me," he said, shrugging slow. His friends kept shooting pool. I tilted to watch them and didn't feel anything.

"You didn't want to be called," I said.

"Well you got me now, woman."

Low took my beer and finished it. I listened for the hooves of his cowboy heart galloping toward me and I heard them. Or maybe it was a dump truck rumbling by, or a train, or the thickening thunder of that storm I was praying for.

What I'm saying: I beat him in a game of pool and let him take me home. What I'm saying: I let him take everything.

Eine Kleine Nachtmusik

Act I

Scene I

(A living room. CAITRIONA and ADAM, married, sit on a couch together. Her legs, thrown over his. ADAM is smoking a cigarette. Light music is playing. Mozart. It is raining, intermittent grumbles of thunder. It is their house. They are alone. Half-empty glasses of wine are on the table next to them. A half-empty bottle too.)

Caitriona
(flirtatiously, tipsily)
I was reading about Mozart's starling. That's the only reason I showed up! I got obsessed with learning all I could about birds, but I was very new to birding. I was embarrassed. I only knew robins and crows. Blue jays. I couldn't tell phoebes and mockingbirds apart until you. They're both gray!

Adam
(pats her leg)
You did just fine.

Caitriona
I still can't believe I married the guy leading the birding tour. What an unbelievably nerdy thing to do. Your binoculars and vest. It was ridiculous!

Adam
(flirting back, putting his hand to his heart in feigned offense)
I'm offended.

Caitriona
(sweetly swats at Adam's leg, readjusts herself)
You are not!

Adam
(shakes his head)
You're right. I'm not.

Caitriona
I thought you were generic because you said the peregrine falcon was your favorite bird. They're the fastest. It's too easy. How lazy of you.

Adam
(laughing, putting his cigarette out in the ashtray on the table)
You're forgetting the common swift. They fly for ten months straight, never touching land. Besides, you're very judgmental. But don't get me wrong! It's sexy on you.

Caitriona
So, okay. It's your turn. Judge me. What's something I do that drives you crazy?
(CAITRIONA leans over, pours more wine in her glass, more wine in ADAM's. CAITRIONA rests against the couch again, drinks.)

Adam
You ask questions like this. Really. You're always pushing to get a rise out of me. You live for danger.

Caitriona
(slinks her legs back from him, holds her wine with two hands)
What's dangerous about asking a question?

Adam
(gulps his wine and finishes it, lights another cigarette)
(ADAM catches a glimpse of his in-real-life wife MINNIE in the audience, front row and

loses his train of thought for a split second. The train rattles, re-centers itself. MINNIE lifts her mouth in the slightest smile. ADAM continues addressing his stage wife, CAITRIONA, who is also his ex-lover from years ago. MINNIE always sits in the front row when she comes to the play, although he wishes she would sit in the shadows so she wouldn't distract him so much. But that's exactly what MINNIE wants. Distraction.)

Um. What's dangerous about asking a question is that you may very well get the answer you want. Or don't want. I could unintentionally hurt you. I don't want to do that.

Caitriona

But I'm tough. I can take it.

(CAITRIONA sees ADAM's wife MINNIE in the front row. MINNIE is wearing a white dress that glows in the dark. CAITRIONA wishes MINNIE wouldn't wear white and sit in the front row. CAITRIONA wishes MINNIE wouldn't glare at her. It's distracting. Yes, CAITRIONA and ADAM dated long ago, but it was only light and fun, not serious. ADAM had been married to MINNIE for years. They had a child together! CAITRIONA had ADAM's abortion in the nineties, but no one knew about that except her and ADAM. CAITRIONA

*and ADAM maintain their deep eye contact
and the rain machine seems to get louder.)*

Adam

You think I'm unaware of your toughness?
You're the toughest woman I know.

*(ADAM maintains deep eye contact with
CAITRIONA, but yes, there's a part of him
that wants to mouth* sorry *to his wife in the
front row. ADAM wants to reassure her that
he's only repeating the lines the playwright
has written for him, for them. MINNIE is a
strong woman! MINNIE is the strongest
woman he knows! He's always lied to MINNIE
about him and CAITRIONA sleeping together
when they were lovers, although he knew
MINNIE didn't believe him. The continued lie
somehow made it true to both ADAM and
MINNIE. He'd stuck to it for so long — their
entire relationship — he could never go back.
And CAITRIONA having the abortion had
erased everything anyway. Poof! Disappeared. There was nothing left to discuss.
He and CAITRIONA weren't in love anymore.
He loves MINNIE. There MINNIE is, sitting
not ten feet away from him across the stage
wash, the fourth wall, through the proscenium
arch. The lights are hot. The theatre is dead-
silent except for the rain machine and the
intense, complicated string music piping out.*

But ADAM is sure he can hear MINNIE breathing.)

Caitriona
(drinking her wine, tucking even further into herself, folding back)
So tell me what I do that bothers you or I'm going to be *really* annoyed.

Adam
(smoking)
We're having such a nice night. Why do you have to ruin it?
(CAITRIONA uses every ounce of theatre training she has, every bit of discipline to focus on ADAM's face, this fake fight. This fake fight not so unlike their real fights. The ones they used to have when they were together. When ADAM would get jealous of her ex-boyfriends stopping by the theatre. The one who brought her roses after a performance; the other one who brought her tulips. ADAM would wonder what man would bring her flowers the next week or the next. CAITRIONA would remind him that she hadn't asked them to bring her flowers. That she couldn't control people. Everyone did what they wanted to do and what the hell could she do to stop it? CAITRIONA swears she can hear MINNIE breathing in the front row. The

man CAITRIONA is dating now is sitting in the shadows like a proper lover. She'd instructed him where to sit, so as not to be a distraction. He is a listener, a good one. Her body warms, thinking of him. Thinking of the forthcoming night with him. MINNIE thinks CAITRIONA wants ADAM, but CAITRIONA has already had ADAM and that was enough.)

Caitriona
(no longer touching Adam)
I'm not ruining anything! I'm asking a simple question. Here, I'll go first. You eat too many crunchy things. That's how I'd write about you in the bird guide. This is an Adam Bird. It's tan to light brown and it wears a lot of flannel and eats too many crunchy things. The noise is grating.

Adam
You leave your wet towels on the bed.

Caitriona
(fanning Adam's cigarette smoke)
You flirt with other women. *And* you smoke too much.
(A snap of thunder from the rain machine. ADAM feels a gentle jump-twitch in his heart. Maybe it's the smoking? A palpitation. He has

311

those. It doesn't worry him. He even looks forward to them sometimes. A muscle-reminder that his heart is beating now and won't always do that. That anxiety roots him, keeps him closer to God, where he should be.)

Adam
(takes one more drag from his cigarette before putting it out)
So I'll smoke less. And who do I flirt with?

(CAITRIONA vividly remembers the night they made their baby. It really was one night and only one night, which adds to the ridiculousness of what they were to one another, what they are, what they continue to be. It was raining just like the rain machine noising offstage. They'd walked home from dinner and ADAM's glasses were wet and foggy so he took them off, set them on the kitchen table. They'd kissed and kissed by the sink, against the stove, in the doorway, down the hall. They hadn't used anything and CAITRIONA had forgotten to take her birth control but didn't mention it. She thought she'd be okay. She forgot to take it often. When she told ADAM she was pregnant he'd gotten the softest, sweetest look on his face. Told her they could keep the baby, raise it together. She'd told him she wanted to go to Los Angeles, see if

she could get some work out there. She wanted to be an actress. A real actress. The timing was bad. She cried and he cried too. Neither of them had experienced anything like that before. The fear, the looming decision, the shadow afterward. CAITRIONA still didn't have any children and maybe it was too late. The baby she didn't have with ADAM would've been twenty years old. Twenty! And now, ADAM had his daughter with MINNIE. CAITRIONA had bought a soft, fuzzy, pink blanket for their baby and a silver rattle. Wrapped it in expensive paper and dropped it off at MINNIE's baby shower before faking sick and leaving early.)

Caitriona
(puts her empty glass of wine on the table)
You flirt with the barista.

Adam
Which barista?

Caitriona
You know which barista.

Adam
Wow, if I knew which barista, *why* would I ask?

313

Caitriona

That is such a stupid question!

Adam

It is not! I want to know which barista you think I flirt with, so I asked!

(MINNIE crosses and uncrosses her legs in the front row. ADAM can smell her perfume. Jasmine, lemons. He and CAITRIONA don't wear any smells when they're working. It's distracting. It's something they've agreed on. They are decidedly neutral. Zeroes. Empties. ADAM looks away from CAITRIONA, then back again. Her beautiful birdlike face, that sharp nose, those dark eyes. Her hair is pulled up, tied on top of her head, sloppily. Casual. They are actors, pretending to be married, pretending to be at home on the stage, pretending the grape juice is wine. CAITRIONA is wearing a pair of her own pajamas, a matching top and bottom, thin stripes. ADAM is wearing a new white T-shirt, a pair of gray sweatpants — MINNIE's favorite lounging outfit of his. Yes, he can definitely smell MINNIE in the front row and maybe he'll say something to her about wearing perfume in the front row, about sitting in the front row in general. He will tell her to sit in the shadows so as not to be a distraction. He will gentle it by telling her how much he loves her, how

314

much he loves that she supports him and comes to the theatre. It's important to him, their marriage. She's very good at making an effort. Yes, he'd loved CAITRIONA but MINNIE, ah MINNIE. He'd made a life with MINNIE for a reason.)

Caitriona
The young one. The young barista.

Adam
I don't know who you're talking about.

Caitriona
The one who was asking you about the birds!

Adam
I think they all know I'm an ornithologist. I've been going to that coffee shop for years.

Caitriona
And you like to brag about being an ornithologist.

Adam
All right. No more wine for you. You're getting mean.
(The low Mozart keeps MINNIE in ADAM's mind even when he looks away from the front

row, even when he gets used to her smell, the glow of her dress, because MINNIE plays the cello. She travels, playing weddings. There is a man in the quartet. The viola player. ADAM believes MINNIE has a crush on him. More than a crush? ADAM worries they've slept together because MINNIE is impulsive. He's already decided if they've slept together he can forgive her. As long as she promises not to travel with the viola player again. As long as she promises it's over. He can forgive her. He knows she has a wild heart. And he's lied to her about CAITRIONA, so yes, he can forgive her.)

Caitriona
I don't want any more wine anyway!

Adam
I never mean to brag about anything.

Caitriona
Wait. What the hell? We've been listening to the same song all night long. "Eine Kleine Nachtmusik."

Adam
I must've accidentally put it on repeat. The same way we keep repeating this fake argument you want to have with me.

Caitriona

I can't deny myself "A Little Night Music."

Adam

You know, I think it translates to "A Little Serenade," but "A Little Night Music" sounds prettier.

(CAITRIONA can still see what she loved about ADAM. His bird-like face. The sharp nose, his dark eyes. He always has great glasses too. A perfect nose for glasses. She used to love seeing him with his glasses off because it was like seeing him naked before she saw him naked. She remembers the first time she saw him naked that night they made their baby. His skinny hips, the dip made right below his belly button, the hair on his chest. He couldn't climb on top of her fast enough. She didn't care about anything else in that moment. How could she?)

Caitriona
(super-annoyed)
See! You're such a show-off!

Adam

What? I Googled it! Wikipedia! *I'm* not an expert! You always jump to conclusions. You take fucking leaps!

Caitriona
(giggling at first, then turning into full-on laughter)
I can't believe we've been listening to the *same* song all night long. Wow, I'm drunk. I forgot to eat.

(MINNIE crosses and uncrosses her legs. CAITRIONA swears she can smell her. Mint? Lavender? She wishes she wouldn't sit in the front row. She wishes she could smell her lover in the shadows. Maybe she'll tell him to wear something with a cedar base. Maybe she'll tell him to sit closer. Maybe.)

Adam
(laughing lightly)
Do you want some eggs? I'll make you some eggs.

(CAITRIONA changes positions, tucks her legs underneath her and crawls toward ADAM. Her stomach jumps knowing MINNIE is right there, watching. She has to climb on top of him and kiss him. It's her job. It's in the script. See!)

(CAITRIONA changes positions, tucks her legs underneath her and crawls toward ADAM. He leans back, she straddles him. She kisses him passionately for several moments.)

318

Caitriona

Yes. I want eggs. You fry them and I'll sit on the counter while you think of all the things I do to annoy you. I'll write them down. We'll make a list! And you can tell me everything you like about the barista too. Is it her nose ring? It's probably her nose ring.

(ADAM says nothing. He just shakes his head and kisses CAITRIONA. MINNIE crosses and uncrosses her legs in the front row. ADAM thinks of the car ride home with MINNIE. What she'll want to eat for dinner. He thinks of their daughter at home with the babysitter. Whether he and MINNIE will make love tonight. Whether either of them will be able to sleep with the white noise of their secrets humming and humming on a loop.)

(The music — the same song on repeat — perfectly timed, finally ends as the lights dim.)

END ACT I

A GIRL HAS HER SECRETS

This works best if you already have a crush on JFK. JFK Jr. will work too. They were both handsome and intelligent and tragic. Icons. This will work best if you have a white robe and can sing "A Fine Romance" and "Diamonds Are a Girl's Best Friend" in a breathy voice. Do it for the troops! You can wear one of those black slip dresses Marilyn Monroe used to wear; you can spend fifty dollars a week on perfume like she did too. You can live in a hotel like she did. Don't marry or fall in love with the wrong men like she did though; these are only crushes. Don't let it go further. Admire his thick hair, how it's old-time parted on the side. A daguerreotype of a Civil War soldier. Notice how different he is from you. How he's leather and you're lace. You can be as girly as a fluffy poodle and you don't have to apologize for it. You never have to apologize for anything feminine or for putting on your best red lipstick only to stay in the house, only to look out your window like William Carlos Williams's young housewife — that crushed *fallen leaf.* The crushes can border on obsessions, but leave them there, in your mind. Watch them, lust after them, fantasize about them, but never fall in love with them because if there's one thing you must know and learn it's that this is not about love, this has never been about love. This isn't about diamonds either. Or beauty or sexiness. This is about being a certain kind of woman, whoever that certain kind of woman is to you. This is one example: Marilyn Monroe. A petal, pale pink. You can also choose Betty Boop. Use your baby voice like Baby Esther. Men are most powerless when a woman pretends to be vulnerable because she is *pretending* and they are not. Be Josephine Baker or Beyoncé or Rihanna. Or Sylvia Plath. And really, aren't we *all* Sylvia? Brilliant, horny, misunderstood? Brain-zapped and punished for our sadness and obsessiveness as our girlishness widens and blooms and blooms and blooms until we fucking split all the way open? Well, here we go! Let's give them what they want. Our rosewater-breath secrets, these parlor tricks.

CREDITS

These stories originally appeared in slightly different form in the following publications:

"The Great Barrier Reef Is Dying but So Are We" previously appeared as a *Platypus Press Digital Short,* 2018.

"Low, Small" previously appeared in *Blue Fifth Review,* 2016 and was a finalist for *Best of the Net 2016* and *Best Small Fictions 2017.*

"A Tennis Court" previously appeared in *Storychord,* 2016.

"Tim Riggins Would've Smoked" previously appeared in *Literary Orphans,* 2013.

"Surreptitious, Canary, Chamomile" previously appeared in *Lime Hawk Literary Arts Collective,* 2014.

"Fast as You" previously appeared in *Synaesthesia Magazine,* 2017.

"Bearish" previously appeared in NANO Fiction, 2014 and was a finalist for *Best Small Fictions 2015.*

"All That Smoke Howling Blue" previously appeared in *Cheap Pop,* 2014; and was republished in *Best Small Fictions 2015.*

"Knock Out the Heart Lights So We Can Glow" previously appeared in *Gigantic Sequins,* 2013.

"Get Rowdy" previously appeared in *The Collapsar,* 2014.

"Re: Little Doves" previously appeared in *The Offing,* 2018 and was a finalist for *Best of the Net 2018.*

"Out of the Strong, Something Sweet" previously appeared in *Paper Darts,* 2016.

"The Lengths" previously appeared in *Counterexample Poetics,* 2014.

"Small and High Up" previously appeared in *Nib Magazine,* 2013 and was republished in *Miracle Monocle,* 2016.

"Bright" previously appeared in *Monkeybicycle,* 2013.

"Rope Burns" previously appeared in *Folio,* 2014.

"The Darl Inn" previously appeared in *Synaesthesia Magazine,* 2014.

"You Should Love the Right Things" previously appeared in *Blackberry Lit,* 2012.

"Crepuscular" previously appeared in *Wyvern Lit,* 2014.

"Two Cherries under a Lavender Moon" previously appeared in *Synaesthesia Magazine,* 2017.

"When It Gets Warm" previously appeared in *Counterexample Poetics,* 2014.

"Boy Smoke" previously appeared in *Counterexample Poetics,* 2014.

"Dandelion Light" previously appeared in *Atticus Review,* 2015.

"Downright" previously appeared in *Split Lip Magazine,* 2016.

"You Got Me" previously appeared in *WhiskeyPaper,* 2014.

ACKNOWLEDGMENTS

Big thanks and love to my agent, Kerry D'Agostino, and to my editor, Elizabeth Kulhanek. Thank you both so much for your encouragement and kindness. For everything! Here's to girlhearts, dreams, and papers under pillows!

Thank you to everyone at Curtis Brown, Ltd. Thank you to everyone at Hachette Book Group and Grand Central Publishing, with special thanks to Linda Duggins, Kristin Vorce Duran, Tareth Mitch, Alli Rosenthal, Alana Spendley, the art department, the legal department, and big love to every beautiful person who makes books happen.

Thank you to the editors of the literary magazines where some of these stories were previously published. Thank you for reading, editing, publishing, and championing my stories.

To the women of the world, thank you.

To you, dear reader, thank you.

To my parents and my brother, thank you. I love you.

To R & A, thank you. Wow, I love you madly. Forever stoked I get to be your mom.

And to Loran — my husband and lover and best friend, the man who keeps me fed and watered like a little plant while I'm working, the man who makes my tea before I ask and who loves me like Jesus does — thank you. Loving you is wild and easy.

INSPIRATIONS

"1979" by Smashing Pumpkins, *1989* by Taylor Swift, "405" by Death Cab for Cutie, Aaliyah, ABBA, Abbi Jacobson, Acts 17:27–28, Adele, *Adventures in Babysitting,* afros, Alabama Shakes, Alanis Morissette, Alissa Nutting, America Ferrera, "And if I perish, I perish," Esther 4:16, Anne Hathaway, Anne Sexton, Annie Lennox, armpit hair, baby animals, *The Baby-Sitters Club, Bad Behavior* by Mary Gaitskill, The Bangles, Banks, *Before Sunrise,* Bessie Smith, "Best Song Ever" by One Direction, The Beverly Hills Hotel, "Bitch Better Have My Money" by Rihanna, "Black" by Pearl Jam, Blondie, The Blossoms, *Born to Die* by Lana Del Rey, bougainvillea, "The Boy Is Mine" by Brandy & Monica, "Brass in Pocket" by The Pretenders, "Brave" by Sara Bareilles, *Break Any Woman Down* by Dana Johnson, "Breathe (2 AM)" by Anna Nalick, Britney Spears, *Broad City,* the Brontë sisters,

"Burn" by Ellie Goulding, "California" by Joni Mitchell, "California" by Phantom Planet, "California Dreamin'," "California Love (feat. Dr. Dre and Roger Troutman)" by 2Pac, "California Nights" by Best Coast, "California Stars" by Billy Bragg & Wilco, "California Waiting" by Kings of Leon, "Candyman" by Christina Aguilera, *Can't and Won't* by Lydia Davis, Carey Mulligan, celebrity crushes, Celine Dion, The Chantels, "Chateau Lobby #4 (in C for Two Virgins)" by Father John Misty, Chateau Marmont, *Chewing Gum,* The Chiffons, Christina Ricci, *Clueless, Conversations with Friends* by Sally Rooney, The Cookies, Courtney Love, "Crimson and Clover" by Tommy James & The Shondells, "Cruel Summer" by Bananarama, "Crush with Eyeliner" by R.E.M., Crystal Wilkinson, The Crystals, daisies, deserts, "Diamonds" by Rihanna, Diana Ross, *Difficult Women* by Roxane Gay, Dinah Washington, Dixie Chicks, The Dixie Cups, Dolly Parton, The Doors, Dorothy Vaughan, Drew Barrymore, *An Education,* Eleanor Tomlinson, "Electric Feel" by MGMT, Elizabeth Barker, Elizabeth Ellen, Elizabeth Winder, Ella Fitzgerald, "Emotional Rescue" by The Rolling Stones, *Empire Records,* Ethel Waters, everyone/everything in "Girlheart Cake with

Glitter Frosting," The Exciters, Exposé, Feist, feminists, *Fleabag*, flowers, "Foundations" by Kate Nash, Françoise Hardy, Free, "Free Fallin' (Tom Petty cover)" by John Mayer, Frida Kahlo, friendship bracelets, Gail O'Neill, *Girl* by Blake Nelson, "Girl" by Frente!, "Girl Almighty" by One Direction, *Girls, The Girls* by Emma Cline, "Girls" by Santigold, *Grease,* Gwendolyn Brooks, Haim, "Hands on You" by Ashley Monroe, Harry Nilsson, *Harry Styles,* "He Thinks He'll Keep Her" by Mary Chapin Carpenter, Hedy Lamarr, "Hey Jealousy" by Gin Blossoms, *Hidden Figures,* "The Hills" by The Weeknd, hippie music, Hole, "Holland" by Sufjan Stevens, *Honeymoon* by Lana Del Rey, hotels, "I Enjoy Being a Girl" by Peggy Lee, "I Feel That Too" by Jessie Baylin, "I'm Every Woman," Idina Menzel, Ilana Glazer, "Impossible" by Mothxr, Incubus, "Independent Women, Pt. 1" by Destiny's Child, "Into the Groove" by Madonna, "It Ain't California" by Kip Moore, "It's in His Kiss," "It's My Party" by Lesley Gore, jacaranda, Jamie Quatro, Jane Kenyon, Janet Jackson, Jasmine Guillory, Jenny Slate, Jesus Christ, Jimi Hendrix, Joan of Arc, John Hughes, "Just a Girl" by No Doubt, "Just Like Heaven" by The Cure, Kacey Musgraves, Kate Bush, Kate

Mara, Katherine Johnson, "Kiss Me" by Sixpence None the Richer, Koko Taylor, "Last Goodbye" by Jeff Buckley, Lauryn Hill, "Leather and Lace" by Stevie Nicks and Don Henley, Led Zeppelin, Lisa Bonet, Liz Phair, Lola Kirke, Loretta Lynn, "Losing You" by Solange, "Love Is a Battlefield" by Pat Benatar, "Lover Lay Down" by Dave Matthews Band, *Lovesick, Lovesong, Loving, Loving v. Virginia,* "Lovely Rita" by The Beatles, *Lust for Life* by Lana Del Rey, Maggie Gyllenhaal, "Man in Space" by Billy Collins, Mandy Moore, Mariah Carey, Marilyn Monroe, Martha and the Vandellas, The Marvelettes, Mary J. Blige, Mary Jackson, Mary Wollstonecraft, Maya Angelou, Megan Stielstra, menstrual cycles, Michelle Obama, *Middle Cyclone* by Neko Case, "Mint Car" by The Cure, Miranda July, moms, moons, "Mother Mother" by Tracy Bonham, "My Boyfriend's Back" by The Angels, "My Funny Valentine," "My Wandering Days Are Over" by Belle & Sebastian, Nancy Sinatra, Naomie Harris, "Naughty Girls (Need Love Too)" by Samantha Fox, Neil Young, *New Girl,* Nina Simone, *Normal People* by Sally Rooney, Olivia Wilde, The Orlons, pearls, Peggy Lee, *PEN15,* peonies, perfume, Petra Collins, "Pillowtalk" by Zayn, Pink, *Plan Coeur,*

"Playground Love" by Air, poetry, "Praying" by Kesha, *Pretty Woman*, Rachel McAdams, rainbows, Rashida Jones, "Retrograde" by James Blake, "Right Hand Man" by Joan Osborne, Rissi Palmer, Robyn, The Rolling Stones, *Romeo + Juliet*, Rooney Mara, Ruby Bridges, "Run the World (Girls)" by Beyoncé, "Runaround Sue" by Dion, The Runaways, Ruth Negga, Sade, Salvation Mountain, Sam Cooke and Muhammad Ali singing "The Gang's All Here," Samantha Irby, Sandra Bullock, Sarah Vaughan, *Sassy* magazine, *A Seat at the Table* by Solange, *Secretary*, "The Seed (2.0) (feat. Cody ChesnuTT)" by The Roots, *Sex and the City*, "Sexy Sadie" by The Beatles, The Shangri-Las, "She Works Hard for the Money" by Donna Summer, The Shirelles, "Sister Golden Hair" by America, skateboarders, Sleater-Kinney, "A Song for You" by Gram Parsons, Spice Girls, "Spin the Bottle" by Juliana Hatfield Three, "Summertime" by The Sundays, stars, "Stay (I Missed You)" by Lisa Loeb, "Strawberry Fields Forever" by The Beatles, summer, "Sweet Thing (feat. Chaka Khan)" by Rufus, "Sweet Thing" by Van Morrison, "Take On Me" by A-ha, "Teenage Dirtbag" by Wheatus, "Teenage Dream" by Katy Perry, "Tell Me Something Good (feat.

Chaka Khan)" by Rufus, Terry McMillan, "thank u, next" by Ariana Grande, "That's Not My Name" by The Ting Tings, *Thelma & Louise,* "Thinkin Bout You" by Frank Ocean, Timothée Chalamet, TLC, *To All the Boys I've Loved Before* by Jenny Han, Toni Collette, Toni Morrison, "Torn" by Natalie Imbruglia, *Towelhead* by Alicia Erian, Tracee Ellis Ross, "True Affection" by Father John Misty, "Truth Hurts" by Lizzo, Uma Thurman, Vampire Weekend, Vanessa Hudgens, Veruca Salt, "Visions of Johanna" by Bob Dylan, "The Way You Look Tonight," "We Didn't" by Stuart Dybek, "We Found Love (feat. Calvin Harris)" by Rihanna, "West Coast" by Coconut Records, "West L.A. Fadeaway" by Grateful Dead, "What a Fool Believes" by The Doobie Brothers, "What Do Women Want?" by Kim Addonizio, "Where Are You Going, Where Have You Been?" by Joyce Carol Oates, "Where Have All the Cowboys Gone?" by Paula Cole, *Who Will Run the Frog Hospital?* by Lorrie Moore, "Wild Ones" by Kip Moore, *Wildflowers* by Tom Petty, Winona Ryder, "Wonder" by Natalie Merchant, "Work" by Rihanna, "The Year I Learned Everything" by Roxane Gay, "You Don't Own Me" by Lesley Gore, "You Know I'm No Good" by Amy Winehouse, Zawe Ash-

ton, Zelda Fitzgerald, Zoë Kravitz, Zora
Neale Hurston . . . etc., etc., etc.

ABOUT THE AUTHOR

Leesa Cross-Smith is a homemaker and the author of *Every Kiss a War* and *Whiskey & Ribbons*. She lives in Kentucky with her husband and children.

Visit her on Facebook: LCrossSmith; Twitter: @LeesaCrossSmith; or Instagram: @LeesaCrossSmith.